As they moved on, [...]
unnaturally quiet. The birds, the squirrels, even the insects were still, as if all of nature were holding its collective breath. The tension was contagious. Fargo shucked the Henry from its saddle scabbard and rested the stock on his leg.

Suddenly Lucy drew rein and extended her arm toward a dense cluster of Sitka spruce. "I saw something move!" she whispered.

"What was it?" Fargo asked, bringing the Ovaro to a stop next to the Palomino.

"I can't rightly say. But I think it was on two legs."

"You think?" Fargo tucked the Henry to his shoulder and kneed the stallion forward a few yards. He estimated they were well over a mile from the meadow. It was doubtful the warriors had overtaken them, let alone circled around in front of them without him being aware of it.

"See anything?" Lucy nervously asked.

Fargo shook his head. He was about to chalk it up to her imagination when he glimpsed a pair of dark, fierce eyes fixed on him from within the undergrowth. . . .

THE TRAILSMAN

#232

PACIFIC PHANTOMS

by

Jon Sharpe

A SIGNET BOOK

SIGNET
Published by New American Library, a division of
Penguin Putnam Inc., 375 Hudson Street,
New York, New York 10014, U.S.A.
Penguin Books Ltd, 27 Wrights Lane,
London W8 5TZ, England
Penguin Books Australia Ltd, Ringwood,
Victoria, Australia
Penguin Books Canada Ltd, 10 Alcorn Avenue,
Toronto, Ontario, Canada M4V 3B2
Penguin Books (N.Z.) Ltd, 182–190 Wairau Road,
Auckland 10, New Zealand

Penguin Books Ltd, Registered Offices:
Harmondsworth, Middlesex, England

First published by Signet, an imprint of New American Library,
a division of Penguin Putnam Inc.

First Printing, February 2001
10   9   8   7   6   5   4   3   2   1

The first chapter of this book originally appeared in *Salt Lake Siren*,
the two hundred and thirty-first volume in this series.

① REGISTERED TRADEMARK—MARCA REGISTRADA

Printed in the United States of America

PUBLISHER'S NOTE
This is a work of fiction. Names, characters, places, and incidents either are the
product of the author's imagination or are used fictitiously, and any resemblance to
actual persons, living or dead, events, or locales is entirely coincidental.

The Trailsman

Beginnings . . . they bend the tree and they mark the man. Skye Fargo was born when he was eighteen. Terror was his midwife, vengeance his first cry. Killing spawned Skye Fargo, ruthless, cold-blooded murder. Out of the acrid smoke of gunpowder still hanging in the air, he rose, cried out a promise never forgotten.

The Trailsman they began to call him all across the West: searcher, scout, hunter, the man who could see where others only looked, his skills for hire but not his soul, the man who lived each day to the fullest, yet trailed each tomorrow. Skye Fargo, the Trailsman, and the seeker who could take the wildness of a land and the wanting of a woman and make them his own.

Oregon, 1861—when deadly spirits haunt a mining town, it's up to the Trailsman to put them to rest . . . permanently.

1

The big man in buckskins had no idea he was being watched as he reined up beside a swift mountain stream. Swinging lithely down from his pinto stallion, he stretched, flexing his broad shoulders. He had been on the trail for days, and his muscles were stiff from riding. As his piercing lake-blue eyes roved over the stately ranks of Douglas fir that covered a nearby slope, a jay squawked at him from its roost high up on a branch. Elsewhere in the shadowed depths of the woods a squirrel chattered.

Skye Fargo smiled as he sank onto a knee and removed his hat. The western half of the new state of Oregon was a lush wilderness largely unexplored by whites. Just the sort of verdant paradise he liked most, where a man could lose himself for days and weeks on end, living off the land and generally doing as he pleased without anyone to tell him different.

Bending, Fargo dipped his hand into the cold, clear water and cupped some to his mouth. It tasted delicious.

He was traveling west over the Cascade Mountains and in another day or so would reach the Willamette Valley, his destination. In his back pocket was the letter that had brought him. That, and the promise of five thousand dollars. At the moment he was practically broke and badly needed the money.

Dipping his hand into the stream again, Fargo froze at the distinct metallic rasp of a rifle lever. Someone had come up behind him, his stealthy tread drowned out by the gurgling water. If this stranger had intended to kill him, Skye rea-

1

soned, he could have done so from ambush, so evidently he wanted Skye alive. For the moment, at least.

"Don't move, mister," a gruff voice demanded. "We don't aim to harm you, but me and the boys will put windows in your skull if you make a play for that six-shooter on your hip."

Now Fargo knew there was more than one. He sensed rather than heard someone idle up close enough to snatch his Colt and step back again.

"Stand up and turn around," the spokesman ordered. "Nice and slow, if you please. You can put your hat on, but keep your hands where we can see 'em."

Fargo did as he was told, Four men had guns trained on him. The apparent leader was a big-boned character in homespun clothes and scuffed black boots, the Colt now wedged under his wide brown leather belt. Beside him stood a lean fellow with a nose as long as a buzzard's beak and an Adam's apple the size of a horseshoe. The third man was a grizzled oldster whose faded buckskins had seen much better days. The fourth, to Fargo's mild surprise, was an Indian, a short, stocky mass of muscle in a high-crowned black hat, dusky skin and brown shirt, his raven hair cropped just below the ears.

A Modoc, Fargo guessed. It was rare to encounter them so far north.

"Who might you be, friend?" the leader asked. "And what in hell are you doing in this neck of the woods?"

"I don't see where it's any business of yours," Fargo responded good-naturedly enough.

They didn't strike him as being run-of-the-mill cutthroats. He assumed they had an excuse for what they were doing and he was willing to hear them out so long as they didn't start anything.

"That's where you're wrong." The man in homespun encompassed the surrounding mountains with a sweep of his arm. "This land belongs to Luther Brunsdale. Maybe you've heard of him? He's one of the richest, most powerful gents

2

in all of Oregon. And he don't cotton to folks traipsing over his property as they see fit."

"He owns all this?" Fargo was impressed. There had been nothing in the letter to indicate how vast Brunsdale's holdings were.

"And lots more, besides. Some say he has the biggest stretch of prime timberland between the Columbia River and Sacramento."

"Lucky him," Fargo said dryly.

"Luck had nothing to do with it. Mr. Brunsdale laid claim to all this country pretty near twenty years ago. He's worked hard to make the Brunsdale Timber Syndicate what it is today. The newspapers call him a timber baron and say he's carved out a regular empire."

"You work for him, I take it?"

"We all do. I'm Tom Poteet. Ordinarily I work as a flume herder, but Mr. Brunsdale has a lot of us out beatin' the brush, huntin' the vermin who murdered over a dozen people so far."

The older man in buckskins gestured. "Quit your jawing, Tom. How do we know this coon ain't in cahoots with them? I say we take him down to the line camp. Dinsmore will know what to do."

"I reckon you're right, Grizwald," Tom Poteet said.

The skinny man had been admiring the Ovaro the whole time, and now he moved toward it, saying, "I claim the horse. My feet are plumb wore out from all this hiking around." He reached for the reins.

"No!" Fargo said, taking a step.

Instantly, the four men tensed, Grizwald training a Sharps on his sternum, the Modoc taking a bead squarely on his forehead.

"I beg your pardon?" the stringbean said, seeming amused.

"No one rides my animal but me," Fargo stated. It was the principle of the thing. On the frontier a man's horse was as much a part of him as his clothes, and it was unthinkable for anyone to use another's mount without permission.

"Is that a fact?" Smirking, the skinny man grabbed the reins anyway.

"I won't tell you twice," Fargo warned.

Tom Poteet turned to the smug troublemaker. "Maybe it's best if you don't, Oddie. No sense in givin' this gent a hard time until we know who he is and what he's doing in these parts."

"I told you," Oddie said, moving next to the saddle, "I'm tuckered out. I'm a bucker, not a damned bull whacker. I'm not used to all this walking. It won't hurt if I ride down to the line camp." He grabbed the saddle horn and lifted a boot to the stirrup.

Fargo tensed, waiting for the explosion sure to follow. The stallion didn't take to being ridden by strangers, as Oddie learned a heartbeat later when the pinto nickered and reared, knocking Oddie backward.

"Damn you!" Compounding his stupidity, Oddie held on to the reins, which incited the Ovaro into prancing to one side to pull free. In doing so, the stallion stepped in front of Grizwald and the Modoc.

It was the opening Fargo needed. A long bound brought him to Tom Poteet and he drove his right fist into Poteet's gut. He regretted slugging the man, but he had the Ovaro to think of. As Poteet buckled, Skye yanked on the Colt, pivoted, and slammed the barrel against the side of Oddie's head with enough force to crumple Oddie where he stood. Another bound, and he was astride the pinto and cutting sharply on the reins.

Grizwald had lowered his Sharps and started to run around in front of the stallion. Caught flat-footed, he was battered aside, lost his balance, and fell.

That left the Modoc, who moved in closer and elevated his rifle. A flick of Fargo's leg swatted the barrel aside just as the man squeezed the trigger. The slug meant for him whizzed harmlessly into the forest canopy, and before the Modoc could fire again, Fargo was across the narrow stream

4

and in among the Douglas firs, riding hell-bent for leather while bent low over the saddle.

"Stop him!" Poteet yelled.

A rifle boomed but Fargo had veered to the left and the bullet clipped a branch a yard away. Within moments he was out of their sight, and safe, bearing westward. He heard Oddie and Grizwald cussing up a storm, their outbursts rapidly fading as he held to a gallop for the next quarter of a mile.

Convinced no one was after him, Fargo slowed to a walk and assessed the situation. He saw no reason to change his plans. Now that he had an inkling of why he was needed, it was more important than ever he find the man who had sent for him.

The blazing afternoon sun was warm on Fargo's face as he descended a wooded slope to a grassy shelf that afforded a sweeping vista of the foothills below, and gave him his first glimpse of the Willamette Valley miles beyond. For decades now, the fertile valley had lured Easterners by the thousands with its promise of prime farmland for the taking. To them, Oregon was the Promised Land, and they were more than willing to endure the severe hardships of the Oregon Trail in order to see that promise fulfilled.

About two miles to the northwest, smoke from a campfire curled skyward. The line camp, Fargo guessed, and rode on down over the rim toward it. The letter had not been all that specific about how to reach Brunsdale's; the men at the line camp were bound to know,

The firs were replaced by madrones, ash, and pines. Thick undergrowth limited the range of Fargo's vision, and he rode with his hand on the butt of his Colt. After what the four men had told him, he had to be ready for anything.

In a quarter of a mile the vegetation thinned at the border of a high-country meadow sprinkled with bright-yellow flowers. Butterflies flitted breezily about, and several doe grazed along the tree line.

Drawing rein, Fargo scanned the meadow carefully. It wouldn't do to venture into the open until he was sure he wouldn't be ambushed. He was about to tap his spurs against the stallion when movement at the far end of the meadow alerted him to a rider approaching from across the way. Possibly another of Brunsdale's men, he thought, until the rider emerged from deep shadow into the brilliant light of day.

It was a woman, a tall blonde whose golden locks cascaded over her shoulders in luxurious curls. She had high, full cheekbones, an oval chin, and red lips as full and inviting as ripe cherries. Only in her early twenties, she had on a green riding outfit complete with a matching wide-brimmed green hat, and was mounted on a magnificent Palomino with a flowing mane and tail. Her saddle was the best money could buy, a fancy affair studded with enough silver to make a *vaquero* drool with envy.

Intrigued by the woman's beauty, Fargo was content to let her cross toward him rather than risk scaring her off by showing himself.

Humming to herself, the blonde was idly gazing down at the yellow flowers, not at the forest where she should. She was about midway when a hint of motion above her drew Fargo's gaze to a glittering shaft streaking out of the air.

"Look out!" Fargo bawled, whipping his reins and hurtling from the trees.

Startled, the blonde glanced up just as the arrow struck her saddle. Narrowly missing her thigh, it imbedded itself in the pommel, causing the Palomino to rear. Although the woman clutched at the horn, she was pitched backward and fell, landing on her back in the high grass. She leaped right back up but her mount was fleeing to the south.

Another arrow arced out of the blue, thudding into the ground an arm's length from where she stood.

"Get down!" Fargo shouted, but the blonde did no such thing, She saw him rushing toward her, and in her confusion she apparently assumed he was somehow to blame for her plight. She whirled and ran—away from him, toward the very spot where the arrows were coming from.

"No! I'm trying to help!" Fargo yelled, but he was wasting his breath. The woman was making for the trees with the speed of an antelope, her tanned face twisted toward him.

Off in the forest a shadowy shape materialized.

"Watch out! In front of you!" Fargo roared, pointing.

Finally, the blonde heeded him and faced the wall of vegetation just as another shaft was loosed. The arrow flashed toward her heart like a bolt of wooden lightning. Fargo thought for sure she was a goner. But almost at the last split-second she hurled herself forward onto her stomach, her hat flying off as she dived, and the shaft pierced her hat instead of her body.

Palming the Colt, Fargo banged off two swift shots at the archer. Whoever it was melted into the greenery, and before another arrow could be fired, Fargo reined to a halt beside the winsome beauty and extended his hand. "Hurry! Up behind me!"

To her credit the woman didn't argue. Springing erect, she grabbed his wrist and permitted him to hoist her onto the saddle, her long arms wrapping tight around his waist. "Get us out of here! Where there's one there are usually more!"

As if to prove her right, out of a thicket to the north of the first bowman flew two more arrows, whizzing toward the Ovaro.

"Hang on!" Fargo exclaimed, hauling on the reins. Both shafts missed. Applying his spurs, he felt her full bosom mold against his shoulder blades and caught a tantalizing whiff of her musky perfume. He raced after her Palomino, which had just disappeared into the forest to the south.

The woman's breath fluttered warmly on the nape of Fargo's neck and he found himself thinking of her enticing full red lips when he should have been concentrating on the task of staying alive.

No more arrows were fired. The stallion gained the sanctuary of the woods without further mishap but Fargo didn't slow until they had traveled a couple of hundred yards. He lost sight of the frantic Palomino, which was still fleeing at a breakneck pace.

Reining up, Fargo wheeled the pinto to check their back trail. "I don't think they're after us. "

"First Julius, now Caesar!" the woman declared, staring in the direction her mount had gone.

"Ma'am?" Fargo absently asked while extracting cartridges from his gunbelt to replace those he had used.

"The Palominos my father gave me for my birthday four years ago. Julius was stolen by the savages a month ago, and now poor Caesar might be badly hurt!"

"You named your horses after an old Roman?" Even Fargo had heard of the renowned leader of old, but he chuckled just the same.

"What's wrong with that?" the blonde said a trifle indignantly, "I love to study history, Roman history in particular. Julius Caesar was one of the greatest leaders who ever lived. I'd wager he was every bit as big and broad-shouldered as you."

"If you say so," Fargo said to be polite. Done reloading, he twirled the Colt into its holster and trotted on after her horse.

"I'm Lucy Brunsdale, by the way. I gather that you are one of my father's men?"

Fargo looked over his shoulder. Up close she was even more stunning, her eyes as blue as the deepest spring, her teeth snowy white. He imagined running his tongue over them, then chided himself for behaving like an awestruck sixteen-year-old. "No, I'm not."

A wariness crept over Lucy's features and she eased several inches back. "You're not? I'd assumed you were. My father doesn't like strangers roaming our land."

"So I've heard."

"Who are you? What are you doing here?"

Fargo introduced himself, thinking her father would have mentioned him, but Lucy plainly had never heard his name.

"Don't misunderstand, mister. I'm grateful for what you did. You saved my life, and my father will reward you handsomely."

"Any idea who I saved you from?" Fargo inquired. It had to be Indians, but to the best of his recollection, none of the tribes in Oregon were on the war path.

"We call them the Phantoms."

Fargo looked over his shoulder again and arched an eyebrow.

"I'm serious. No one knows who they are or why they're killing people. About five months ago it started. The Carter brothers were doing a timber survey for my father and didn't return when they should have. So a search party was sent out. Both men had been horribly butchered in their tents." Lucy placed her hands on his shoulders. "Since then fourteen people have died. The only clues have been moccasins prints and a few arrows left in the bodies."

"Someone must know which tribe it is," Fargo insisted.

"Shows how bright you are. No white man has ever set foot in this region before. The trappers shunned it because there aren't enough beaver to speak of. Ranchers want nothing to do with it because there's not enough good graze for their cattle. And the farmers can't be bothered to clear trees for farming when there's plenty of prime farm elsewhere for the taking."

"Did anyone question friendly local tribes?"

"As a matter of fact, yes. The Calapooyans are the closest. They live down in the Willamette Valley. They say this area is bad medicine, that their people never come up here. My father talked to their chief and the chief is as stumped as we are."

"What does the army say?"

"They're next to worthless. Fort Hoskins is the only post within hundreds of miles. My father sent a rider to ask for help and the army sent a patrol under Captain Barker. He's been scouring the mountains for weeks now and hasn't turned up a thing."

The whole affair sounded peculiar to Fargo but he decided to reserve judgment until he learned more. A whinny up ahead alerted him they had caught up to the Palomino, and he spotted the animal in heavy brush, its dangling reins tangled fast.

"Caesar!" Lucy exclaimed, pushing off the Ovaro. She ran to the horse and lavished kisses on its neck. "Oh, Caesar! I was so worried. I couldn't bear to lose you after losing Julius."

Fargo couldn't help thinking how enjoyable it would be if he were the object of her affection. Climbing down, he examined the arrow imbedded in the pommel. It hadn't gone all the way through. Grasping the ash shaft, he wrenched upward and out came a barbed point similar to those used by tribes along the coast. The feathers were from an eagle. He hoped to find markings that would identify the tribe or owner but the shaft was bare.

"I hope you won't hold this against me," Lucy Brunsdale said.

"Hold what?" Fargo said, rotating, and stared into the muzzle of a derringer, "Is this how you show gratitude?"

"I don't think you're out to harm me. I honestly don't. But a gal can't take needless chances, can she? Undo your gunbelt and hand it over. I promise you'll get it back soon."

Fargo was tired of people pointing guns at him. He slowly lowered his left hand to his buckle, and then, while she was watching him pretend to loosen it, he lashed out with the arrow, smacking it hard against her wrist, so hard she yelped in pain and involuntarily pressed her forearm to her stomach. Seizing her wrist, he twisted it none-too-gently. Again she yelped, and dropped the derringer.

"Damn you! My father will gut you for this!" Lucy's other hand speared at his eyes, her fingers hooked to claw and rend.

Sidestepping, Fargo shifted his hold on the arrow so the barbed point was inches from her bosom, "Don't tempt me."

Lucy's cheeks flushed a vivid scarlet and she balled her fists. "If I were a man, I'd box your ears in!"

"A lot have tried," Fargo mentioned, pointing at the Palomino. "Now climb on. You're taking me to your father."

"Like hell I am," Lucy replied. "It'll be a cold day in hell before I do anything for you." She folded her arms across her chest.

"Maybe you'd rather I stab your horse?" Fargo bluffed.

"You would hurt Caesar?" Lucy blurted in horror as she threw her arm up over the animal's neck. "I misjudged you. I gave you the benefit of the doubt, but you're no better than the Phantoms."

"If you say so." Fargo picked up the derringer, stuffed it into a pocket, and forked the Ovaro. "Daylight is wasting. Don't keep me waiting."

Grumbling under her breath in a most unladylike manner, Lucy stepped into the stirrups and headed to the northwest.

"Hold it," Fargo said. It was his understanding the Brunsdale place was due west, at the base of the foothills flanking the Cascades. "Your home is that way." He nodded.

"My father isn't there," Lucy said, continuing on. "He's at the line camp overseeing the hunt for the Phantoms." She paused. "How is it you know so much about my family all of sudden? You've never been to our place before that I know of."

"Everyone knows about your father and his famous Timber Syndicate," Fargo said. Which wasn't entirely true. He had never heard of Luther Brunsdale until the letter arrived, but then, he seldom read a newspaper and had little interest in big business and high finance.

"They think they do," Lucy said with unaccountable bitterness.

"You don't sound all that happy about the empire he's created," Fargo casually observed, quoting Tom Poteet. Anything to keep her talking and take her mind off how mad she was at him.

"I was five when my father brought us out here," Lucy revealed. "My mother didn't want to leave Ohio, but he insisted, so like a good little wife she obeyed. We weren't here a year when she died."

"Life on the frontier is rough," Fargo conceded. Especially for women, who toiled at backbreaking chores from dawn until dusk, day in and day out, year after year, until their bodies were stooped from wear and tear and their hair turned gray before their time.

"It wasn't that. My mother died of a broken heart. She hated Oregon and wanted to go back to Ohio, but my father refused. By then the syndicate had been formed, and he couldn't very well leave his investors in the lurch, now could he?"

The crack of a twig reminded Fargo of the attack in the meadow. Lucy heard it, too, and reined up and looked at him. "We'll swing to the west to be safe," he whispered. "No more talking."

Lucy didn't argue. For a quarter of an hour they threaded through alders, oaks, and more madrones. Once they flushed a long-eared rabbit that sped off in gigantic leaps, spooking the skittish Palomino. It neighed and acted up, snorting and dancing until Lucy brought it under control.

As they moved on, Fargo noticed the woods were unnaturally quiet, The birds, the squirrels, even the insects were still, as if all of Nature were holding its collective breath. The tension was contagious. Fargo shucked the Henry from its saddle scabbard and rested the stock on his leg.

Suddenly Lucy drew rein and extended her arm toward a dense cluster of Sitka spruce. "I saw something move!" she whispered.

"What was it?" Fargo asked, bringing the Ovaro to a stop next to the Palomino.

"I can't rightly say. But I think it was on two legs."

"You think?" Fargo tucked the Henry to his shoulder and kneed the stallion forward a few yards. He estimated they were well over a mile from the meadow. It was doubtful the warriors had overtaken them, let alone gotten around in front of them without him being aware of it.

"See anything?" Lucy nervously asked.

Fargo shook his head. He was about to chalk it up to her imagination when he glimpsed a pair of dark, fierce eyes fixed on him from deep within the undergrowth, One instant they were there, the next they were gone, but there was no mistaking them for anything other than what they were.

Reining the pinto around, Fargo bellowed, "Back! Back the way we came!"

As Lucy hauled on the Palomino, an arrow buzzed out of nowhere and sank into the bole of a spruce almost at her elbow.

Swiveling, Fargo fired at where he had seen the eyes. Another shaft clipped the whangs on his right sleeve. A third came close to transfixing the Ovaro's neck. With a slap of his legs, he shot out of there, puzzled that the warriors never whooped, never showed themselves. It was almost as if he were fighting Apaches, but that couldn't be. He was over a thousand miles from their haunts in Arizona and New Mexico.

The Palomino pounded up a short slope and Lucy cut to the left. Fargo would rather have gone to the right, but he let her do as she wanted in the belief she knew the countryside better.

The next second a rifle cracked, and Lucy Brunsdale cried out and pitched from the saddle.

2

Skye Fargo swiveled toward the thicket the shot came from and fired three times as swiftly as he could work the Henry. He was rewarded with a strident cry, then the crash of brush. Drawing rein, he sprang from the saddle and dashed to Lucy. She lay on her stomach, her golden hair askew, unmoving.

To stay there invited another attack. Since the Palomino had kept on going, Fargo quickly brought the Ovaro over and shoved the Henry into the scabbard. Tucking at the knees, he carefully rolled Lucy Brunsdale over, slipped his arms underneath her soft, supple body, and lifted. Blood was oozing from a nasty gash on her left temple. How serious it was remained to be seen.

Clambering onto the saddle took some doing, but Fargo succeeded and immediately rode eastward, back up the mountain toward the stream he had stopped at earlier. He needed water, and he figured that by now Poteet and the others were long gone.

The stallion was tired, but rose to the challenge as it always did, climbing briskly until they emerged from the trees to find the stream right in front of them.

Swinging a leg over the horn, Fargo slid down and gently lowered Lucy onto grass growing at the water's edge. She groaned and stirred but didn't revive. Unfastening his red bandanna, he soaked it in the stream, wrung it out, and gingerly cleaned the bullet wound. It was an inch and a half long and about an eighth of an inch deep. Thankfully, the slug had merely creased her. She would have a scar, but she would live. Curling his legs, Fargo sat and repeatedly dampened her brow and cheeks to keep her cool.

The forest around them was deathly still for a while, but soon the chirping of sparrows and the cawing of a raven assured Fargo they were alone and temporarily safe.

Lucy's lustrous hair framed her angelic features in a shiny halo. She was breathtakingly beautiful, the kind of woman who would turn every male head on any street in any city in the country. In repose her full bosom rose and fell rhythmically. Her red lips, the lips Fargo so admired, were parted invitingly, and he could see the pink tip of her tongue between her pearly teeth.

A constriction formed in Fargo's throat. Over two weeks had gone by since he'd last savored the charming company of a willing woman, and he indulged in carnal thoughts of doing the same with her.

Leaning toward the stream to wet the bandanna again, Fargo looked down and discovered her eyes were open and she was regarding him rather strangely. "Don't try to get up," he advised. "You've been shot."

"Who—?" Lucy said, as if she didn't recognize him. Abruptly, she did exactly as he had just suggested she shouldn't do, and tried to rise. Grimacing in torment, her eyelids fluttering, she sank back down with a pitiable mew.

"Some people never listen," Fargo quipped, wringing out the bandanna.

"My head," Lucy said thickly. "It's pounding. It hurts terribly."

"You're lucky you're still breathing," Fargo said. "Another quarter of an inch to the right and you would be worm food." He pressed the bandanna against the furrow. "We'll rest here until you're strong enough to ride."

"I remember everything now!" Lucy said, her eyes darting to either side. "Where's Caesar?" Again she attempted to stand. Again raw agony washed over her and she sank onto her back, too weak to lift a finger. "'I feel dizzy. And sick to my stomach."

"You will for a while but it will pass," Fargo said. "As for Caesar, he ran off. I'll go hunt for him, if you want, after we get you home."

Lucy's gaze bored into him like twin drills. "Why are you being so kind after I've treated you so shabbily? After I pulled a gun on you?"

Fargo grinned. "A woman can't be too cautious these days. I don't hold it against you. Just don't try it again."

"Did you see who shot me?"

"No. I was more concerned with getting you out of there."

"No one has had a good look at a Phantom yet," Lucy said. "They come and go like ghosts, melting into the shadows whenever anyone gives chase. Even our best tracker, Modoc Jim, hasn't been able to catch one."

Fargo remembered the stocky Modoc with Tom Poteet. "We're quite a ways north of Modoc country," he noted.

"I wouldn't know. Modoc Jim showed up at the settlement about, oh, four months ago. Rem Dinsmore, my father's right-hand man, ran into him and hired him on the spot. Modocs are fabulous trackers."

"So I've heard," which made Fargo wonder how Modoc Jim had been unable to trail the so-called Phantoms to their lair. Something wasn't quite right but he didn't have enough facts to say what it was.

Closing her eyes, Lucy reached up and plucked at his sleeve. "Oh my. The dizziness is getting worse. "

Fargo clasped her hand, her palm warm on his. "It will go away eventually. Maybe it's best if you don't talk for a while."

"Are you kidding?" Lucy mustered a wan smile. "My father likes to tease me that I couldn't shut up if my life depended on it." She grit her teeth for a few seconds. "You could be right, though. I'd better just lie here. Sorry."

"For what? Being shot?"

Lucy started to giggle, then winced. "Consarn you, Don't make me laugh. It hurts too much."

Folding the bandanna into thirds, Fargo soaked it through and through and placed it on her smooth brow. After a while her chest resumed its rhythmic rise and fall. He was content to sit there, protecting her, as the sun sank by gradual degrees toward the western horizon.

Fargo was beginning to feel drowsy himself, when the blonde gave a start and sucked in a deep breath.

"Oh! Goodness gracious! How long was I out?"

"A couple of hours," Fargo told her. "It will be dark in another three or so. If you're not up to traveling by then, we'll spend the night here."

"The two of us? Alone?"

"I'll behave if you will." But it would take a lot of self-control, Fargo mused.

"No, it's not that. The nights aren't safe. The Phantoms are always abroad after dark. It's actually rare for them to be out and about during the day, as they were today." Lucy sighed. "Just my luck. The first time in ages I get to come up here and the damn Phantoms are all over the place."

"I'm surprised your father let you go riding alone," Fargo said.

"He would throw a fit if he knew. I wasn't supposed to leave camp unless I took some guards along, but I didn't want any company so I snuck off when no one was looking."

"Not very wise," Fargo said bluntly.

"I was tired of sitting around twiddling my thumbs," Lucy responded. "Back before this whole Phantom business started, I came up here riding all the time."

"You say it's rare for the Phantoms to be out during the day?" Fargo said. "How rare, exactly?" Few tribes raided at night. Some believed that warriors who died in the dark could not find their way to the spirit world. For others, it was a matter of custom and common sense. At night an enemy was

17

harder to find and hard to fight. And at night predators were on the prowl for prey.

Lucy thought a bit. "This is the first time I know of. Isn't that a bit odd?"

It was extremely unusual, but Fargo refrained from saying so for the time being. "Care for a bite to eat? I have some pemmican in my saddlebags."

"Pemmican? What's that?"

Fargo thought she must be joking. How anyone could live on the frontier for seventeen years and not have hard of pemmican was beyond him. Rising, he brought her a handful. "Courtesy of a Shoshone woman. It's made from dried buffalo meat, pounded into fine pieces, then mixed in with fat and crushed berries." Done right, pemmican could last for years without spoiling.

Lucy accepted a piece and sniffed it. "Smells a little like jerky." Nibbling, she chewed a while, swallowed, and smiled. "Why, it's downright delicious."

"Venison and beef can be used, too."

"Teach me how before you go. It would be great to take up in the hills when I ride." Lucy frowned. "That is, once the Phantoms are disposed of."

Fargo sat, draping his forearms across his knees. "Do you like living here?"

"Not all that much, no. It's a lonely life. My social circle consists of a few close friends down to the valley. Farmers' daughters, mostly, who are never quite comfortable around me because I'm Luther Brunsdale's daughter." Lucy touched her temple. "If I had my druthers, I'd live in St. Louis or New Orleans or maybe New York. I prefer city life to country living."

"You're old enough to strike off on your own if you want," Fargo commented.

"Would that I could! My father and I have argued endlessly about it and the result is always the same. If I move out on him, he'll disown me. I won't receive a cent to live off of, and he'll cut me off from my inheritance."

"You value money more than freedom?"

"I'm practical, is all. Show me a sane individual who would rather be poor than rich. I like my creature comforts and I apologize to no one for it."

"Creature comforts aren't everything."

"Easy for you to say. You weren't reared in the lap of luxury, as folks say. You aren't accustomed to the finer things in life. Asserting my independence isn't worth living the rest of my days as a pauper."

Fargo thought just the opposite. To him, being free, being able to do as he pleased when he pleased, was everything. A life without freedom was an empty existence.

"I can tell by your expression you don't necessarily agree," Lucy said. "Well, to each their own. One day I'll get my wish, though. Wait and see. My father will come around to my way of thinking. He always does. I'll get to live in the city of my choice in fine style."

Unexpectedly, from the woodland below came the crackle of undergrowth. Fargo sprang erect, palmed his Colt, and moved to a spruce. Peering past it, he spied over a dozen men hastening upward. In the lead was Modoc Jim, glued to the Ovaro's tracks. Fargo also recognized Tom Poteet, Grizwald, and Oddie.

"Who is it?" Lucy whispered as he holstered the revolver and backed from the tree.

"Your rescuers have arrived."

A minute later the Modoc appeared, advancing cautiously. When he spotted Fargo, he halted and said something to someone following him.

Out of the pines strode a huge bearded bear in a narrow-brimmed brown hat, a beige woolen work shirt, striped suspenders and baggy pants, and thick boots. Over his left shoulder rested the long handle of a double-edged axe. "Lucy!" he cried. Racing up, he dropped onto a knee and clutched her hand in both of his. "I was worried sick! Tom and the boys said they saw a stranger, and then we heard shots—" The man saw her wound and stopped, aghast. "You've been shot!"

"Yes, Rem," Lucy said. "But I'm—"

Rem Dinsmore wasn't listening. Surging upright, he swung toward Fargo, his knobby knuckles wrapped around the axe handle. "You did this! You're just as they described you!" And with that, he swept the razor-edged axe on high.

Fargo was caught off guard. He had expected to be thanked for saving the woman's life, not set upon by an enraged colossus. Throwing himself to the left, he barely avoided a downward stroke that would have cleaved his head in half.

"Rem, no!" Lucy screamed, but it did no good.

Dinsmore was beside himself with fury. He swung again, aiming the axe at Fargo's midsection.

Jerking backward, Fargo saved himself a second time. He saw the blonde struggling to stand but she would be too late to help. Left with no choice, he drew the Colt, his thumb curling around the hammer and cocking it as he cleared leather. He shoved the barrel almost in the logger's face.

Rem Dinsmore, set to wade in again, turned to stone.

"Drop it or die," Fargo said.

Tom Poteet, Grizwald, and Oddie were fanning out, all with their guns leveled. "You're the one who will buck out in gore, mister, if you don't lower that hog-leg!" Poteet threatened.

Fargo was not about to do any such thing, not with the walking mountain ready to chop him off at the waist.

That was when another man rushed out of the forest. In his late forties, he was dressed in the height of fashion, in a suit that cost more than most loggers earned in a year. A straw skimmer crowned his graying hair, and he carried an ivory-handled cane. "Enough!" he commanded with an imperious air of unquestioned authority. "Rem, put down that axe! Tom, you and the boys will lower your guns!"

Lucy had gained her feet but she was swaying like a reed in the wind, her hand over the gash. "Father!" She took a step, groaned loudly, and passed out.

Luther Brunsdale went to catch her but someone else beat him to it. Rem Dinsmore dropped the axe, spun in a blur, and cushioned her in his enormous arms with a gentleness that was remarkable to behold.

"I have her, sir." The huge logger glared at Fargo. "This bastard shot her. Why did you stop me from splitting him down the middle?"

"It looked to me as if I stopped him from blowing your brains out," Luther Brunsdale said, and faced around. "Who are you, stranger? I demand to know what you're doing on my property."

Fargo lowered the Colt but he didn't holster it just yet. Poteet, Oddie, and some of the others looked fit to blast him into eternity at the least little provocation. Fishing in his back pocket, he pulled out the folded envelope containing the letter he had received and gave it to the timber lord. "The Phantoms hurt your daughter, not me. Here. This will explain everything."

Luther Brunsdale accepted it, blinked a few times, then shocked everyone by grasping Fargo's arms and yipping with glee. "Skye Fargo! You came! I can't thank you enough!"

The timber men exchanged puzzled glances. Rem Dinsmore's bushy eyebrows met above his nose and he said, "Fargo? The one they call the Trailsman? You sent for him, boss, without telling anyone??"

"I sure did!" Brunsdale crowed, wrapping an arm around Fargo's shoulders as if they were long-lost brothers. "I sent a letter off over a month ago care of the post commander at Fort Laramie, To be honest, I never really expected it to reach him. It was a long shot but it paid off."

"How so, sir?" Tom Poteet asked. "What makes this jasper so special?"

"He has a reputation for being one of the best trackers in the country," Luther Brunsdale declared. "They say he learned from the Sioux. That he can track an ant over solid rock. An exaggeration, I'll grant you, but he's gone up against the likes of the Comanches and Blackfeet and lived to tell about it, which is more than most can say."

"Sounds like one tough hombre," Grizwald said.

Fargo didn't much like how they were talking about him as if he weren't there. "I usually get the job done," he said, shrugging loose. "And I take it the job you have for me is to track down these Phantoms, as you call them?"

"That's it in a nutshell," Luther Brunsdale said. "Where the Hanken clan and Modoc Jim have failed, I'm counting on you for results."

"The Hanken clan?"

Rem Dinsmore answered before his employer could. "Farmers down in the valley. Hill folk from Tennessee who did a lot of hunting before they migrated to the Oregon Country. They've got themselves a coon dog, and they're the best damn trackers around."

How was it then, Fargo pondered, that they, like the Modoc, had failed to bring the Phantoms to bay? There were a lot of questions he needed to ask, but they could wait for a more suitable time and place.

"Let's save the small talk for later," Luther Brunsdale said. "Right now we must attend to my daughter. Oddie, I want Slim, Ted, and you to go on ahead. When you get to camp, take three horses and ride like the devil down to the settlement. Tell Doc Stephens I want him up here as soon as he can make it."

"Will do, sir," Oddie said, and lit out of there as if shot from a cannon, the other two Brunsdale had mentioned hard on his heels.

Dinsmore, however, wasn't ready to let the issue drop. "Why bring in an outsider, sir? We can handle our problems on our own. All we need is a little more time."

"Time?" Brunsdale virtually spat. "It's already been half a year and you're no closer to stopping the Indians than you were when you started. Fourteen people have died, with no end to the slaughter in sight, and you want more *time*?" Brunsdale angrily gestured. "We've dallied long enough. My daugh-

22

ter comes before all else. Rem, you carry her. Modoc Jim, go on ahead and ensure a war party isn't lying in wait. Grizwald and Salzman, bring up the rear. We don't want them picking any of us off from behind like they did to the flume crew."

Fargo liked how the timber baron exercised command, doing exactly what needed doing. "You missed your calling. You should have been an army officer."

Luther chuckled. "You're not the first to say so. I'm afraid, though, army fare is a far cry from steak and lobster. And army pay is less than I pay my maid." He clapped Fargo on the back and started down. "I can't begin to express how glad I am you came."

"I have a fair notion." Taking hold of the stallion's reins, Fargo fell into step beside him.

"Not really." Brunsdale lowered his voice so no one could overhear. "Just between you and me, Mr. Fargo, I'm at my wit's end. My timber empire is on the verge of ruin. A lot of decent, hardworking people have lost their lives, and hundreds more are in danger of losing their lives. And why? Because a band of Indians no one has ever heard of and no one can catch evidently feel I've intruded on their land and they're doing all in their power to put me out of business."

Fargo made mental note of yet another peculiar tidbit of information he would delve into later.

"I find it virtually inconceivable," Brunsdale had gone on. "But I'll be damned if I'll let them get away with it." He gripped Fargo's wrist. "Before I go any further, let me make one thing perfectly clear. I know you've lived with Indians on occasion, so it wouldn't surprise me if you were sympathetic to their cause. But as God is my witness, I've never harmed a red man in all my life." He removed his straw skimmer and ran his hand through his graying hair. "Which makes my predicament all the more aggravating. If I had known there were Indians living up here, I'd have made every effort to contact them before I sent my crews in."

"You've been logging for seventeen years, I hear," Fargo mentioned. "And you never had trouble like this before?"

"Never. To my knowledge these mountains were uninhabited. Even the Calipooyans, who live down in the valley, had no idea a tribe claimed this land."

Fargo was fairly familiar with the distribution of the tribes in the region, To the north, along the broad Columbia River, were the Yakimas, Klickitats, and others. To the northeast dwelled the famed horse breeders, the Nez Perce, while to the southeast lived the Klamaths and the Bannocks. Far to the south was Modoc country. Nearer were the Rogue River Indians, whose uprising had been put down a few years ago. And along the Pacific Coast were dozens of other tribes.

Fargo knew of only two who lived in Cascades, the Wintu and Nomlaki, neither of whom dwelled in that particular area. He could understand why Brunsdale was so perplexed.

"The last thing I need is Indian trouble," the timber baron said. "Not when my operation is running so smoothly, when I'm literally making money hand over fist."

The trees opened before them, affording a view of the distant Willamette Valley.

"When I first came to Oregon back in '43, there were a thousand people living there, if that," Brunsdale said. "Each year since then the population has grown by leaps and bounds. Now it stands at over fifty thousand, and twice that many will flock here by the turn of the century."

"That's a lot," Fargo said, without enthusiasm. It was yet another example of how the wild places he loved were slowly being eroded away by the incoming tide of settlers.

"All of them need homes. All of them need places of business. In short, they require lumber, finished wood by the ton, a ready-made market for the right man in the right place."

"And you're that man."

"I foresaw the demand long before anyone else. While others scoffed, I built the first sawmill and carted wood on up the valley in rickety old wagons. It paid off. That first year

I netted a profit of seven thousand dollars, Sounds like a lot of money, but now I earn that much in a week."

Suddenly the five thousand Fargo was to receive for his services didn't seem like all that much.

"Of course, my costs have risen as my empire has grown. Where once I had four men on my payroll, now I have four hundred. Where once I paid barely a hundred dollars a month to my partners in the Syndicate, now I pay over twenty thousand."

"Tell me more about this Syndicate of yours."

"There's not much to tell. I needed capital to start my logging concern, and my uncle and a friend put up the money in return for a share of the profits and a vested interest in managing things." Brunsdale looked at him. "It's all perfectly legal, if that's what you're thinking. My uncle and I were always close. He looked after me when my father died. Were it not for him, I never could have made the move from Ohio to Oregon."

Below them Dinsmore had stopped. Lucy Brunsdale had recovered and was steadying herself with her slender hand on his barrel chest.

"She's come around!" Luther scampered down in excitement and enfolded her in his arms. Lucy sagged against him and he stroked her hair in an excess of fatherly affection.

Only Fargo caught the fleeting spite that rippled across the roughhewn features of their trusted foreman.

"Do you have any idea, daughter, how worried I was when Caesar came trotting into camp by himself," Luther chided her. "I was giving Rem a tongue-lashing for letting you slip off after I had given him specific instructions to safeguard you."

"Don't blame him," Lucy said. "I snuck off on my own."

"It's still Rem's fault. He should have known you would try one of your little stunts and taken appropriate precautions." Luther held her at arm's length. "You're deathly pale. I'll have the men rig a litter."

"I refuse to be babied," Lucy said. "I can make it on my own."

"In a pig's eye," Luther responded, and turned toward the waiting loggers.

Fargo stepped forward. "I have a suggestion. She can ride double with me. I'll take her on ahead to the line camp and wait for you."

"An excellent idea!" Luther said, and without delay guided his daughter toward the Ovaro.

Not everyone agreed. A minute later, as Fargo clucked to the pinto and headed lower with the blonde's arms wrapped around his waist and her cheek on his shoulder, he glanced back at the brooding form of Rem Dinsmore.

If looks could kill, he would be as dead as dead could be.

26

3

The logging camp was typical of others Skye Fargo had seen.

In addition to a score of canvas tents, half a dozen shanty buildings had been erected, including a long bunkhouse and the most popular building of all, the cookhouse. A handful of horses were kept in a crude corral, and oxen were everywhere. Usually they would be hitched in teams out in the tall timber, hauling logs, but the attacks by the Phantoms had ground work to a standstill, Over fifty roughhewn men were standing around with nothing to do.

North of the camp was a flume thirty feet high, supported by a sturdy trestle. From it came the rumble of logs on their way down the mountain to the sawmill.

To say Fargo and Lucy's arrival caused a stir would be an understatement. The loggers stopped whatever they were doing and flocked toward the Ovaro. By the time Lucy Brunsdale told Fargo to rein up in front of a building at the very center of camp, they were surrounded by dozens of burly timber men, many eyeing Fargo suspiciously.

Lucy dismounted without help and faced the loggers. "It's all right, men! This man is a friend! He's been hired to track down the Phantoms. My father and the foreman will be along shortly and explain everything."

"What happened to you, Miss Brunsdale?" an onlooker anxiously asked.

"One of the Phantoms winged me," Lucy reported, then indicated Fargo. "This gentleman saved my life."

Murmuring broke out, and heartfelt oaths were cast toward the encircling woodland. It was plain the loggers despised the Phantoms, and equally plain they adored their employer's daughter. They pressed forward, talking all at once.

"Is there anything we can do for you, Miss Brunsdale?"

"Would you like some ointment, Miss Brunsdale?"

"How about if the cook makes you some tea, Miss Brunsdale?"

Raising her arms, Lucy smiled. "I'm fine! Don't fret! Mabel will patch me up good as new. You can get on with your work."

"What work?" a man in overalls responded. "Your pa won't let us leave camp until those miserable redskins are taken care of."

As the loggers began to disperse, Fargo climbed down and looped the Ovaro's reins around a hitch rail. "Did you know your father sent for a doctor?"

"He did? When I was unconscious?" Lucy wasn't pleased. "He shouldn't have done that. Old Doc Stephens has enough to do."

The door opened and out bustled a rather prim young woman in a brown dress with a splash of white lace at the throat. An apron adorned her slim waist. Her brunette hair was done up in a bun, and she wore plain brown shoes that would do a Quaker proud. "Miss Brunsdale! I thought I heard your voice!"

"Mabel, I'd like you to meet a friend." Lucy introduced Fargo.

The brunette, it turned out, was a maid. "She's only been with us about half a year but we've become fast friends," Lucy said, giving Mabel a squeeze. "She's from Ohio, from Cincinnati, where I was born."

"Small world, isn't it?" Mabel said, smiling. Then she saw the wound. "What in the world! We're standing here jabbering while you need tending? Let's get you inside." Mabel

28

whisked Lucy through the doorway and went to close the door.

"Skye, too," Lucy said. "He's my father's guest, and they'll have a lot to discuss when father arrives."

"Oh?" Mabel replied.

"Yes. He's here to save us from the Phantoms."

Mabel studied Fargo with renewed interest. "You don't say? And you honestly think you can succeed, sir, where so many others haven't?"

"I'll try my best," Fargo said, sauntering in. A modestly furnished parlor was flanked by a narrow hall. At the other end were several doors.

Lucy was being steered to a settee. "Don't mind this place, Skye. It's not much, but father insists on roughing it when we're out in the woods."

Fargo glanced at the plush rug on the floor, at the polished bronze lamps and an easy chair that could double for a royal throne. "You call this roughing it?"

"Compared to our house this place is a hovel," Lucy said. "It doesn't even have an indoor pump."

Mabel hustled down the hall and was back within moments with a blanket. "To keep you warm, miss," she said, laying it across Lucy's lap and down her legs. "I'll be back with bandages in two shakes of a lamb's tale." Out she hastened once more.

"Isn't she a dear?" Lucy said. "She fusses over me like a mother hen. My last maid, Mrs. Edlemeyer, was an old crone in her sixties who never cracked a grin and treated me as if I were a child."

"Do you have any brothers or sisters?" Fargo asked, making small talk.

"I wish. My father wanted more children, but my mother had such a hard time of it with me, they decided not to." Lucy leaned back. "Mother nearly died in labor. Doc Stephens had to help things along, if you take my meaning."

Fargo sat down in a rocking chair in the corner, removed

his hat, and placed it on his knee. "Tell me more about the Phantoms."

"There's not much more *to* tell. They live back up in the mountains somewhere, shut off from the rest of the world, even from other tribes, All the men they've killed were shot from ambush."

"Tell me about the men, then."

"Let's see. There have been fourteen. Did I mention the Carter brothers were the first to die? I did, didn't I? They were surveyors, and they were east of here about five miles, camped by a small lake. Apparently the Indians snuck up on them while they were in their tent. About a week later, the warriors killed Fred Harman, a bull whacker who had gone into the forest after a bull that strayed from camp. He was found with four arrows in his back."

"Go on."

"Must I? Do you have some sort of morbid fascination with death?"

"It will help me," Fargo said. Sometimes it was possible to tell a lot about a tribe by the manner in which they slew their enemies. Apaches, for instance, were fond of torturing victims to test their courage. Some tribes cut out the tongue, or the eyes, or indulged in some other type of mutilation.

"Well, then, let me think," Lucy scratched her chin. "After Fred there were three buckers who—"

"Buckers?" Fargo interrupted.

"When a big tree is felled, the buckers split it into shingle bolts. Three of ours were working north of the flume. They failed to show up for supper so Rem went looking for them. Two had been riddled with arrows, just like Fred Harmon, and the third man had his skull caved in."

"Did they have guns with them?"

"They had a rifle, yes. Father insisted all the workers go armed after Fred was killed. The third man tried to reach it but was caught before he could."

"And the rest?"

"Let me see. Two were choker setters, one was a skid

greaser, a sweet kid only fifteen years old, and there were four plume herders."

"That's thirteen," Fargo noted.

"It is? Oh. I almost forgot. One of the Hanken boys was killed. My father hired them to track the Phantoms down, and Bobby Hanken, the oldest son, was shot through the heart." Lucy frowned. "I liked him. I think he was fond of me, but he was too bashful to admit it. Whenever I went to the settlement, he would bring me flowers." She pressed a hand to her head. "What's keeping Mabel? My head is hammering again."

Fargo glanced toward the hall and saw a shadow silhouetted on the opposite wall. Someone was just around the corner, eavesdropping, He was about to rise to see who it was when the shadow moved and into the parlor came Mabel. She was carrying a sliver tray. On it were a washcloth, clean white bandages, and a bottle of liniment,

"There you are!" Lucy said.

"Sorry, Miss Brunsdale. It took me forever to find the liniment," Mabel apologized, setting the tray on a small mahogany table.

Fargo had learned all he was going to from Lucy. "I think I'll take a stroll around the camp," he announced, standing.

"Must you?" Lucy asked, and when he nodded, she said, "Before you go, promise me that you'll join us for supper this evening at seven. In addition to her other talents, Mabel is a wonderful cook." She beamed at the brunette. "What are we having tonight?"

"Roast venison. One of the loggers shot a buck this morning and gave an entire haunch to us."

"Wasn't that kind of him?" Lucy said. "The men always go out of their way to be so nice. I swear, every last one of them must think of me as his sister."

Fargo suppressed a laugh. Loggers were notorious for spending most of their earnings in brothels, not for being saints. Donning his hat, he said, "I'll take you up on your invite." He smiled at Mabel and she returned the favor, but he detected a certain coldness in her gaze. That wasn't uncommon. Women on the frontier had to take extra care not to be too friendly or they acquired a reputation for being forward. And from there it was a short hop, skip, and a bedsheet to be being branded a loose woman.

"Don't forget. Promptly at seven," Lucy said.

The loggers were scattered throughout the line camp in huddled clusters. Fargo drew curious stares as he roved among the buildings and tents, glad to stretch his legs. From the cookhouse wafted tantalizing odors that made his stomach growl. He peeked in the bunkhouse, which was empty, and was moving along a row of tents when heavy footsteps came up behind him.

"Hey, you!"

Fargo turned to confront five men in shabby, well-worn clothes. An elderly man was in the lead, his jaw jutting in anger and his bony fists clenched. The others ranged in age from about thirty down to fifteen or sixteen. Their features were uncannily similar, giving Fargo a clue as to who they were.

"What's this we hear about Mr. Brunsdale sent for you to track for him?" the older man brusquely demanded, his Southern accent thick enough to cut with a knife.

"You must be the Hanken clan," Fargo said.

"That we are, mister," the patriarch declared. "I'm Seth Hanken. These here are my boys, Orville, Harry, Josiah, and Theodore."

"Lucy Brunsdale told me about your other son, Bobby."

"Don't remind me." Seth Hanken shook his fists in impotent rage. "Those filthy heathens. They killed my boy! They knew he was the one man they couldn't shake, so they crept in close one night and shot him dead as he was stepping from the cookhouse."

"Wait a minute," Fargo said. "He was killed here in camp?"

"Don't you have ears?" Seth spat in ill-concealed contempt. "The Phantoms are always out there spying on us."

Fargo surveyed the woods. "I'll find them. And when I do, whoever murdered your son will pay."

"You won't be finding anybody," Seth stated. "We want you to get back on that pinto of yours and hightail it somewhere else."

"You're serious?" Fargo said, more amused than angry at their gall.

"My pa taught me a man should always say what he means and mean what he says," Seth replied. "Hell yes, I'm serious. My boys and me are going to hunt the Injuns down without any help from you or anyone else."

"Luther Brunsdale hired me—" Fargo began, but Seth did not let him finish.

"He hired us, too. But he hired us before he hired you. Paid us five hundred in advance, with a promise of five hundred more once we get the job done. And we're not about to let you or anyone else cheat us out of our rightful due."

"We can work together—" Fargo tried again, with the same result.

"The Hankens do their own work, mister. You'd only get in our way. So we're asking you, nice and polite-like, to climb on the hurricane deck of that cayuse of yours and light a shuck for wherever your heart desires. So long as it ain't after the Injuns." Seth paused. "What do you say?"

"Go to hell."

Seth Hanken's mouth opened wide enough to admit a swarm of flies. "Are your ears plugged with wax? I just explained how things are. You don't have any choice in the matter."

"You've got that backwards," Fargo said. "I've agreed to help Brunsdale, and that's exactly what I'm going to do. For your own sakes, don't get in my way or there will be hell to pay."

Cackling, Seth looked at his sons. "Do you hear this coon, boys? He talks mighty big, doesn't he? Maybe he reckons we're all bluster and brag. Maybe he thinks all he has to do is talk tough and the Hankens will back down." Seth motioned. "Teach him the error of his ways, boys. Beat him within an inch of his life and throw him on that stallion. "

Fargo's hand swooped to his Colt but he didn't draw; he realized none of the Hankens were armed, not even with a knife.

The oldest, Orville, waded in with his arms spread wide, intending to grapple him to the ground, but Fargo had other ideas. Cocking both fists, he adopted a boxer's stance, and when Orville awkwardly lunged, he ducked and planted an uppercut that rocked Orville on the heels of his boots. A right to the chin sent him crashing back against Josiah and Theodore, and all three went down.

"Get him, Harry!" Seth bellowed. "Don't let him make fools of your idiot brothers thataway!"

Harry was a wiry specimen who must have learned some boxing himself somewhere along the line. He skipped in with his fists waving in front of his face like tree limbs in a gale. His stomach, though, was unprotected, and Fargo sank a left into the pit of his gut that doubled him in half and left him sputtering and wheezing like a bellows.

"Damnation!" Seth fumed. "Did I raise men or sissies?" Grabbing hold of Orville and Josiah, he shoved them. "Get in there and wallop the tar out of this pilgrim."

Fargo stiffened to meet their rush, but they had learned from their mistakes. Instead of barreling toward him like two buffalo gone amok, the brothers slowed and separated, craftily circling to either side.

"You done hurt me, mister," Orville "For that I aim to pound you."

Not to be left out, Josiah exclaimed, "Me, too!"

Word of the fight was spreading through the camp like wildfire and loggers were rushing to witness it, forming a ring around the combatants. One man bawled, "I've got ten dollars that says the Hankens come out on top!"

"You're on!" another responded.

In his travels Fargo had seen many a brawl and taken part in more than his share. He had found that victory didn't always go to the strongest or the swiftest, but to the savviest. "Fight smart," a seasoned veteran of saloon mayhem once told him, and it was just about the best advice he had ever been given. Now, as Orville and Josiah prepared to spring, he put the advice to the test by doing the last thing they expected. Rather than wait for them to attack him, he tore into them.

Fargo took two quick steps and flicked a combination that jolted Orville. Instantly, he pivoted to meet the youngest, who had leaped toward his back. A solid right flattened Josiah. By then Harry and Theodore were closing in, Harry with his head lowered like a charging bull, Theodore looking none too sure of himself but propelled forward by a push from his father.

"Fifteen dollars on the Hankens!" a logger hollered, waving the bills.

"I've got twenty on the stranger!" another man declared.

Fargo avoided Harry by skipping backward, then thrust his left leg out, catching the Tennessean across the shins. Harry tripped and fell onto his hands and knees. Furious, he heaved up off the ground and inadvertently collided with Theodore, who had marshaled the gumption to rush in. Both wound up in a tangled heap, Harry swearing in livid abandon.

Seth Hanken was hopping up and down in a fit of apocalyptic proportions. "Don't just lie there! Where's your grit? Your grandma could do better than you boys are. Get up and hit him! Hit him hard!"

Orville rose, thunder on his brow, "I'll fix his hash, Pa!" he cried, windmilling his fists.

Fargo retreated, luring him in, letting Orville expend his energy in a flurry of useless blows. Then, when Orville paused to catch his breath, Fargo drove his right fist past the man's guard, his knuckles connecting with Orville's lower ribs.

Orville folded, but Harry and Josiah were right there to take his place. Shoulder to shoulder they hurled themselves at Fargo's legs, and before he could leap aside, they tackled him and bore him to the dirt.

"Now you've got him!" Seth howled. "Gouge his eye! Break his fingers! Bite him where it hurts most!"

Fargo glanced down, and damned if Harry wasn't opening his mouth to do just that. He slammed his knee against Harry's ear, and when Harry reared back, he tucked his left leg to his chest and catapulted his boot into Harry's stomach. The impact flung Harry against Josiah, spilling them both at their father's feet.

"Worthless! That's what you no-accounts are! Worthless!" Seth commenced kicking his own sons. "Get back up and make me proud!"

Pushing erect, Fargo braced for their next attempt.

Just then a commotion broke out among the loggers. They parted to the right and left as through their ranks stormed a blond she-cat with her claws unsheathed. "How dare you!" Lucy Brunsdale snapped at Seth Hanken. "Who do you think you are, assaulting a guest of ours?"

Seth was too flabbergasted to speak.

"Don't deny it! I heard the ruckus and stepped outside, and Caleb Whitney told me what was happening." Marching up to Seth, Lucy jabbed her finger against his chest. "I should have you tied to a log and tarred and feathered for this outrage."

"But—" Seth bleated.

"But nothing! Mr. Fargo was invited here at my father's specific request." Lucy jabbed him several more times. "I want you and your boys out of camp within five minutes. You're never to set foot on Brunsdale property again. And you can forget tracking the Phantoms. We're not paying you another cent."

"You're firing us?" Seth said.

"Yes!"

Fargo couldn't let that happen. "I'd rather you didn't," he interjected.

Lucy and all the Hankens glanced at him in amazement.

She was confused and it showed. "But they assaulted you. They tried to run you off. Why on earth do you want me to go easy on them?"

Fargo had his reasons, but he would rather keep them to himself. Foremost was the fact they were the only ones at the line camp he could completely trust. "I can't explain right now," he said, "but I would like them to work with me."

"You would?" Seth asked, stupefied.

"You would?" Lucy echoed, and flung her hands up in exasperation. "I don't understand you, Skye Fargo. I just don't understand you at all. But if that's what you want, I'll grant your request." Shaking her head, she started to leave, then rounded on Seth and wagged her finger under his nose. "But I'm warning you, Seth Hanken. If you or your boys pull something like this again, I'll personally do all in my considerable power to make your life as miserable as I can possibly make it. Do we understand each other?"

"Yes, ma'am," Seth said timidly.

Lucy stormed off, the unintentional sway of her lush body riveting every male there except for Seth. The elder Hanken came toward Fargo with his hand outstretched.

"I've misjudged you, mister, and I'm a big enough man to admit it to your face. No hard feelings?"

Fargo shook. "No hard feelings." He knew Seth meant it. Hill folk were a hardy, honorable breed. Although quick to anger, they were as honest as the year was long, and their word was their bond.

Seth's four sons were slowly rising, rubbing their bruised and battered bodies. Where Lucy Brunsdale had been confused, they were utterly dumfounded. Even more so when their father gestured and said, "What are you lunkheads waiting for? Shake Mr. Fargo's hand and apologize for how you behaved."

"Us?" Orville blurted. "You're the one who told us to whale him silly. Why should we say we're sorry?"

Harry bobbed his chin in agreement. "Orville's right, Pa. If anyone should apologize, it's you."

Seth placed his hands on his hips. "How would you like to go without vittles for a few days? If your ma hears how you've sassed me, you'll be lucky to get table scraps."

The threat had a noteworthy effect. One by one the younger Hankens filed by, each shaking Fargo's hand and mumbling how sorry they were for the misunderstanding. But the only one who sounded sincere was Theodore.

"Now then," Seth said when they were done, "what is it you want us to do?"

"Be ready to ride out when I need you," Fargo said, and when they reacted as if he had asked them to swallow sour milk, he said, "You do have horses, don't you?"

"A plow horse," Seth said. "An old swayback that's two steps shy of the grave." He brightened. "But we don't need mounts. The Phantoms never use them, so we don't have to bother."

"Never?" Fargo said.

"Not that I know of, no, sir. They're not very bright, these Injuns. Hell, they didn't even have the brains to steal the horses of the men they killed."

"Interesting." Disturbing doubts had gnawed at Fargo for hours now, doubts the latest revelation turned into a firm conviction. "But maybe they have more brains than you give them credit for."

"How do you figure?"

Fargo answered the question with one of his own. "Which is easier to track, a man or a horse?" Leaving the Hankens to ponder his remark, he headed for the hitch rail to attend to the Ovaro.

Lucy and Mabel were in front of the Brunsdale's, the maid holding a bandage and pleading for the blonde to listen to reason.

"Please, miss. That wound can become infected if you're not careful. Your father will never forgive me if I don't bandage it."

"If it starts bleeding again, I'll let you," Lucy said. "Otherwise, quit nagging." She spotted Fargo and used him as an excuse to end the argument. "Skye,! You're just in time. I need to take some air and you're the perfect escort." Sashaying over, she forked her arm around his. "What do you say?"

Mabel, in a huff, trounced inside and slammed the door.

"She means well but she can be such a nag," Lucy said impishly, then shifted so his forearm brushed her bosom. "Now how about that walk?"

Her dazzling smile and lovely features were enough to bend any man to her will, but Fargo hesitated. He wanted to strip the saddle and saddle blanket off the stallion and let it rest awhile. Gazing toward the hitch rail, his attention was drawn to the pines above the camp by the bright gleam of sunlight off metal. He thought it might be Brunsdale's party returning, but it was a lone figure partly hidden by the trees.

A figure who had a rifle pointed at Lucy and him.

4

Skye Fargo reacted instinctively. He shoved Lucy Brunsdale to the left while simultaneously throwing himself to the right. Not a second too soon. The booming retort of the heavy-caliber rifle rumbled across the line camp and a slug plowed into the earth behind them. Fargo saw the rifleman swivel. Pushing to his knees, he hurtled at Lucy, slamming his shoulder into hers and knocking her onto her back.

Again the assassin in the trees fired. Again the slug missed, biting into the dirt at the exact spot Lucy had just occupied.

By now shouts peppered the camp. All eyes swung toward the pines, and within moments loggers were barreling up the slope toward the shadowy figure. A few initially, but in no time at all almost the entire camp was on the move. In a wave the outraged timbermen swarmed toward him, some with weapons but most without, relying on sheer force of numbers to overpower him.

The man in the trees, however, was no longer there. He had wheeled and raced off, the vegetation closing around him.

"You saved my life again!" Lucy cried. "How can I ever repay you?"

Fargo could think of a way, but it had to wait. Running to the Ovaro, he slid the Henry out and joined the raging horde of loggers in their mad exodus. Trying to stop them, to make them realize the blunder they were making, would be pointless so he didn't try.

When Fargo reached the spot where the killer had been,

his fears were realized. Whatever tracks the rifleman had left were being obliterated by over two dozen loggers who had arrived ahead of him and were searching the immediate vicinity, roving back and forth in rampant confusion.

"Stop! All of you!" Fargo hollered, but only a few did. The rest glanced at him as if he were loco.

"What do you want me and my boys to do, mister?"

Fargo had been unaware the Hanken clan had followed him. Seth and his sons were were armed, too, each with an old Kentucky rifle, ammo pouch, and powder horn. "Have Josiah and Theodore do what they can to keep the rest of the loggers back. They're wiping out the tracks." Fargo hurried higher. "The rest of you stick with me."

Based on where the figure had been standing and the direction in which he had fled, Fargo had a pretty fair hunch where to pick up the trail. He passed several loggers rushing aimlessly about, skirted a thorny patch of blackberry bushes in bud, and came to a steep slope dotted by boulders and random madrones. A narrow game trail angled across it, a trail routinely used by deer and other animals on their daily treks to the stream by the flume. On the edge of the trail, in soft dirt, Fargo found what he was looking for. "There!" he said, pointing.

A partial heel print was plain to see, made by a moccasin.

"I'll be switched!" Seth exclaimed. "You're good, friend."

Fargo jogged on. The loggers were well below them, still recklessly blundering about. Seth, Orville, and Harry easily kept up with him, exhibiting the superb stamina for which hill folk were rightfully famed.

On the crest of the slope Fargo halted. The game trail continued to the southeast, but he had spotted a faint smudge that hinted the Phantom had left the trail and entered a belt of ponderosa pine. Diligently scouring the ground ahead, he found a toe print in a tiny square of bare earth. "He went this way."

Seth bent over it and whistled in admiration. "I take back what I said. You're better than good."

"Keep your eyes peeled," Fargo directed. "We don't want to be bushwhacked." He ventured into the ponderosas, deliberately going slow in order not to miss further sign. Murky shadows made the tracking difficult. Here and there he found vague impressions and once another heel print. But all in all, the Phantom was extremely skilled at moving swiftly without leaving much spoor.

The ponderosa pines were thinning when Orville suddenly said, "I think I saw something up yonder."

Fargo raised his gaze from the carpet of pine needles. Another sheer slope loomed, a slope with little cover. Just the sort of spot for an ambush. "Where?"

"In the rocks near the top," Orville said.

Nothing moved that Fargo could see, but that didn't mean Orville was mistaken. "We'll go up one at a time. The three of you cover me until I'm at the top, then I'll cover you."

"Be careful, sonny," Seth said. "These Injuns are meaner than a dog with fourteen sucking pups."

"And they're real partial to backshooting folks," Harry said.

Not always, though, Fargo had noticed. In the past five hours they had made three attempts on Lucy Brunsdale's life, and only once, at the meadow, had they tried to shoot her in the back. They seemed bound and determined to kill her, as if she were of special interest to them. Which made no sense. If the Phantoms were indeed a remote tribe, solely out to defend their territory, why had they singled her out? They had no way of knowing she was Luther Brunsdale's daughter. And if, somehow, they did know, why weren't they after Brunsdale himself?

Some things just didn't add up.

Crouching, Fargo scanned the slope. Then, nodding at the Hankens, he chugged upward, weaving to make himself harder to hit. No shots rang out, and he made it halfway without a mishap. Ducking behind a low bush that wasn't big enough to hide a cat, he scrutinized the jumbled rocks and boulders from end to end but saw no movement.

Digging his soles in, Fargo launched himself higher. He had gone ten feet or so when he experienced the undeniable sensation of hostile eyes upon him. Intuition, some would call it. A sixth sense, others might say. Whatever the case, he had experienced it too many times to discount it. In the wild a person had to learn to trust their instincts, to hone them to a sword's edge. So now, as a prickling sensation broke out at the nape of his neck, he slanted to the right and flattened just as a rifle cracked.

Fargo glimpsed a buckskin-clad shape among the boulders, and he wasn't the only one who spotted it. From the bottom of the slope came answering shots, three in rapid succession, and the Phantom melted from sight.

The Hankens were reloading. Fargo hugged the earth, waiting for them to finish. When Seth glanced up from behind a tree and gestured, he shoved upright and sprinted toward the rim. He covered five yards, ten, fifteen. Another shot pealed off the mountain and a leaden hornet buzzed his left ear. He didn't see the shooter but he heard the Hankens cut loose, and he counted on them keeping the warrior pinned down for the few seconds it took to reach the boulders.

Hunkering with his back to a flat slab, Fargo saw the Hankens reloading once more. With a speed born of long practice, they opened their powder horns and poured the proper amount of black powder down the muzzles of their Kentucky rifles, each knowing exactly how much to add without measuring it. Next they wrapped a patch around a ball and fed it into the barrel as far as their fingers would go. To tamp it down the rest of the way, they relied on the ramrod housed under the Kentucky's barrel. In under thirty seconds they had their rifles cocked and to their shoulders.

Seth started to step around the tree to start up the slope, but he halted when Fargo motioned for him to stay put.

Sliding between the slab and another boulder, Fargo sought sign of the bushwhacker. The boulders were a maze, some as big as a log cabin, most a lot smaller. He wound among them, every nerve on edge, ranging the crest from south to north, and did not encounter the elusive Phantom.

Fargo began to understand why the loggers had bestowed the nickname. Whoever the Phantoms were, their woodcraft was exceptional. They were almost as adept as Chiricahua Apaches, which was saying a lot.

On the other side of the ridge, the slope was rife with pines and choked by dense undergrowth. As Fargo studied its green depths without seeing any trace of the rifleman, another puzzling thought struck him. How was it, he wondered, that warriors who supposedly had not had any contact with whites until recently were so skilled in the use of firearms? Granted, they had stolen a few rifles from the loggers they slew, but how had they learned to *use* them? By watching whites? That seemed unlikely, especially since loggers never used guns except when hunting, and none of the men who were ambushed had been after game at the time.

Yet another aspect of the whole affair that was peculiar, Fargo mused, and mentally rattled the rest off: a tribe no one had ever heard of, not even neighboring tribes; warriors who preferred to raid in the dead of night, which few ever did; killers who had purposely slain the best tracker in camp, Bobby Hanken, and now seemed to have targeted Lucy Brunsdale.

The more Fargo pondered, the more his conviction grew that things were not as everyone assumed. There was more to the Phantoms than seemed apparent, and he intended to unravel the mystery. Too many innocent lives had already been lost.

Winding back through the boulders, Fargo waved, signaling it was safe for the Tennesseans to join him.

Seth, Orville, and Harry ascended the slope with the alacrity of mountain sheep. "Do we keep on after him?" Seth asked.

"We do."

Finding more tracks took a while. The soil was hard-packed and dry. Fargo had to go over the crest twice before he discovered where the Phantom had slipped down into the trees. Once the man had been shielded by vegetation, he had broken into a run.

As always, though, spoor was scant. The warrior had an uncanny knack for setting his feet down where they were least likely to leave telltale prints.

The trail lead to the east. After half an hour of steady tracking, Seth Hanken declared, "Say! I know where we are. My boys and me have hunted up this way. I know what this Injun is up to."

"How do you mean?" Fargo asked.

"You'll see for yourself once we get over this next hill."

The vegetation ended at the edge of a rock field. Loose rocks inches deep blanketed underlying soil as hard as iron.

"Hellfire," Seth said. "The bastard knew just what he was doing. We've lost him for sure now."

"These damn Phantoms never miss a trick, Pa," Orville said. "They ain't hardly human, if you ask me. "

"No one can get the better of them," Harry added.

"We can." Fargo cradled the Henry in the crook of his left arm. "They're human all right. And this one is spooked. He hasn't been able to shake us and he's desperate."

Seth sighed. "We can't track him across ground like this."

"We don't have to," Fargo said. "All we have to do is find where he left the rocks. Seth, you go to the north end. Orville and Harry, to the south. I'll take the east. Give a yell if you find anything."

Fargo headed for the far side at a dogtrot that ate up the acres quickly. Grass bordered the east end, and farther on, more forest. He prowled the area, on the lookout for bent stems. But he had not looked long when a hail from the north drew him to where Seth stood over a moccasin print in the dirt.

"He changed direction on us, sonny. Canny as a fox, these Phantoms. My Bobby almost caught one, though, the day before he was killed. A logger found a few prints near the flume, and Bobby went off alone tracking them. He said he followed the sign for miles but lost it at a stream." Sorrow tinged Seth's face. "Wasn't hardly an hour later that he was shot dead right in front of my eyes."

Orville and Harry hurried up moments later, and Fargo led them anew into heavy woodland. The Phantom apparently assumed they had lost the trail because his tracks indicated he was moving slower than before and taking less care in hiding the prints.

Fargo hiked faster. They were gaining but they were running out of time. The sun had dipped low above the western horizon. At most, they had an hour of daylight left. All the Phantom needed to do was elude them until dark and he was safe.

Tracking at night was possible, but torches were required, and it would limit them to a turtle's pace. The Phantom would get so far ahead, they would have no hope of ever overtaking him.

A comment Seth had made sparked Fargo into glancing back and asking, "How often do you and your sons hunt up here?"

"Once or twice a month," the patriarch said. "You see, back in North Carolina we ate bear meat all the time. It's our favorite, you might say. But bears don't come down into the Willamette Valley much, so we have to come up after them."

"See much Indian sign?"

"Not a lick," Seth answered "You could have bowled me over with a feather when I heard there was a tribe hereabouts. It's like they sprung out of thin air."

"See many other hunters?"

"A few. There's a man named Haskell who lives down to the settlement. He's real genteel. Always carries a handkerchief and sniffs it as if it's a daisy." Seth chortled. "Haskell is from Boston or some such, and he likes to hunt for the sport of it, as he says. Although it beats me how killing critters is sport. We do it to eat."

"Any others?" Fargo probed.

"Just Donovan, the man who does most of the hunting for the timbermen. He used to hunt buffalo on the plains, then his wife dragged him out here to Oregon so she could be near her sister. He has three or four helpers who do the butchering."

"Has he ever mentioned finding Indian sign?"

"No, sir." Seth shook his head. "I remember talking to him about it, and he was as surprised as we were when the Injun trouble began."

Fargo mulled the information. "How far is the settlement from the line camp?"

"Are you fixing to go there and pester the folks there with questions, too?" Seth rejoined. "Brunstown is about a two-day ride from the camp. Brunsdale's big mansion is about halfway between."

"The settlement is named after him?"

"Sure. Why not? It's pretty much run by the Syndicate. There's a general store, a feed store, and a place that sells all the logging gear and equipment the timbermen need. Rumor has it the Syndicate makes quite a profit off every-thing." Seth sounded envious. "Ain't that always the way, though? Those with money keep raking it in, and those with-out keep scrabbling just to make ends meet."

The sun now rested on the rim of the world. Fargo re-luctantly had to admit there was slim hope of success. He pushed on anyway, until the blazing golden orb was gone and gathering twilight mired the woodland in gray gloom. "This is far enough," he announced, halting. Any farther would be pointless.

"Do we pitch camp and begin again in the morning?" Seth asked.

"No. He'll be miles ahead by then. It's best if we go on back and stick close to the line camp."

"Worried about more loggers being killed, huh?"

"Yes." But Fargo was more worried about another attempt being made on Lucy's life. The Phantoms were bound to try again and he needed to be there.

They bent their steps westward, the forest steadily dark-ening around them. For a while birds warbled and chirped as was customary at sunset, then quiet reigned, a quiet so complete that their own footsteps seemed unnaturally loud.

Seth inhaled deeply. "Smell the pines? I love these mountains, friend. Oregon is almost as pretty as Tennessee, and not anywhere near as crowded."

"Is that why you brought your family out here?"

"A man needs stretching room," Seth said. "When I was a sprout, our nearest neighbor was ten miles away. Then more and more people moved in, until my pa packed us up and moved a couple of hundred miles to where there wasn't another living soul. But five years later we were up to our necks in neighbors again. Four times we moved, always to where there weren't any people. Each time, shortly after, more came along and crowded us out."

"Back East folks are breeding like rabbits," Orville commented.

"It's easy living that does it," Seth said. "They've got nothing else to do so they spend all their time making babies. Mark my words. One day there will be so many people, a man won't be able to spit without hitting another man's shoes."

An hour later the lights of the line camp appeared below. Half a dozen campfires and a score of lanterns lit it so brightly Fargo would have no trouble picking off any of the loggers, were he so inclined. Nor would a Phantom. "They're sitting ducks down there," he remarked.

"That they are," Seth agreed. I told Rem Dinsmore as much, too, but it didn't seem to bother him none. He said they're not about to hide in the bunkhouse at night."

No sentries had been posted. Fargo and the Hankens wandered in without anyone challenging them.

"I want to thank you for your help," Fargo said. "Tomorrow we'll go out after the Phantoms again, if you're willing."

Seth pumped his hand. "You'll do to ride the river with, mister, so count us in to the finish. We have to pay the no-accounts back for what they did to my Bobby."

Fargo made for the hitch rail, intending to finally get

around to bedding down the stallion for the night. Then he would apologize to Lucy Brunsdale for missing supper. But as he gripped the reins to unravel them, out rushed the blonde herself, her full figure sheathed in a sleek, satiny dress that accented her shapely contours.

"There you are! We've been holding the meal!" Lucy looped her arm around his. "It's well past eight."

Fargo glanced at the wall of darkness beyond the camp. "You shouldn't be out in the open like this. We didn't catch whoever took a shot at you and they might try again."

"Took a shot at us, you mean," Lucy amended. "And you ran the fellow off so we're safe enough for the time being." She pulled him toward the doorway. "Come on in. Everyone is half starved."

"How's your head?" Fargo asked.

"Just fine." Lucy closed the door. "Mabel made some tea and added a heaping spoonful of laudanum. It's amazing how wonderful I feel."

Not really, Fargo reflected, since laudanum was otherwise known as tincture of opium. One bottle contained enough to make a grizzly woozy. The teaspoon Lucy had been given would have her feeling no pain for hours. Usually, only doctors could prescribe it, and he wondered how it was Mabel had a bottle.

The parlor was empty but not the next room beyond, a cramped dining room dominated by a long hardwood table. Luther Brunsdale was at the head of it, attired in a fine tailored suit, and sipping from a silver goblet. On his left sat Rem Dinsmore and a man Fargo had not seen before, a frail fellow with spectacles who looked as if he would be more at home in a library, among stacks of books. All three rose when Lucy entered and Luther came around the table to greet Fargo.

"Here you are! We heard about the latest incident, and how the Hankens and you went after the culprit. Did you catch him?"

"No," Fargo admitted. "But not for a lack of trying."

Rem Dinsmore was dressed in a store-bought checkered suit that did not quite fit his brawny frame. "So the great Trailsman came up short?" he said sarcastically. "It's like I told you, Mr. Brunsdale. We don't need him. We can handle the Phantoms ourselves."

"Don't start again," Luther said. "I have enough on my mind without you carping about my decision. It's done, and that's that. You will cooperate fully with Mr. Fargo or risk my displeasure. Is that clear, Rem?"

"Yes, sir," the big foreman said sullenly. "It couldn't be more clear if you carved it into my forehead."

"Ignore him," Luther told Fargo. "He's had a little too much wine while we've been waiting."

"If you say so." Fargo was skeptical the wine had anything to do with it.

The timber baron returned to his seat and patted the chair on the right. "The guest of honor always sits here."

Lucy dropped into the chair next to Fargo's, and he saw Dinsmore's jaw muscles twitch. "Wait until you hear the latest, Skye. My father is in shock, and I can't say as I blame him."

"Something to do with the Phantoms?"

Luther Brunsdale answered. "Not at all." He jerked a thumb at the frail fellow in spectacles. "This is Cleve Sneldon, my private secretary. A while ago he brought me the worst news imaginable. A message arrived at my house yesterday morning. My two partners in the Syndicate are about to pay me a visit."

"Your uncle and the other one?" Fargo recalled, mystified by why it upset him.

"My uncle's name is Walter. He's pushing seventy-five, and for him to make the arduous journey from Ohio shows how serious the situation has become."

"You've lost me," Fargo said,

"Walter has never come out here before, although we visited him a couple of times," Luther said. "Not once in the seventeen years I've been managing the daily operation of the company has either man set foot in Oregon. There was never any need. Until this Phantom business started, everything ran smoothly."

"Father is worried they've lost confidence in him," Lucy clarified. "He's afraid they'll remove him as manager."

"They can do that?" Fargo asked.

Luther was refilling his goblet. "That they can," he answered. "Our Syndicate is a partnership, with each partner having an equal say in how it's run and entitled to equal shares of the profits. We signed a binding contract that spells it all out in great detail. And one of the stipulations is that if there ever comes a time when any two of the partners feel the third isn't pulling his weight, they can vote to oust him."

Cleve Sneldon had a mousy voice to match his mousy appearance. "I can't see them forcing you out, sir. Not after the many years of outstanding service you have rendered to the Syndicate."

"I hope you're right," Luther said. "In any event, they're due to arrive in several days. They sent the message from Portland. Lucy and I must head for home tomorrow, and I'd like for you, Mr. Fargo, to accompany us."

"Me?" Fargo said.

"You're an outsider. You have no vested stake in this. If you explain to Walter and Addison Sykes exactly what we're up against, they'll believe you. They'll understand I'm doing the best I can."

"I can do more good here," Fargo stated. A trip to the main house would delay the hunt for the Phantoms by days.

"It's to your benefit as well," Luther said. "If they oust me, I can't pay you. You'll have come all this way for nothing."

Fargo wavered until the decision was made for him by a warm hand on his knee, and slender fingers that slowly slid along his inner thigh to within a few tantalizing inches of his groin.

"If you won't do it for him, do it for me," Lucy Brunsdale said ever-so-sweetly. "And remember, it's not polite to refuse a lady's request."

What else could Fargo say? "What time do we leave?"

5

Lucy Brunsdale had been right. Compared to the Brunsdale estate nestled at the base of the foothills, their place at the line camp was a hovel.

A mansion worthy of a Boston blueblood stood on a low rise. From a broad portico in front Skye Fargo was treated to a sweeping vista of the verdant Willamette Valley. Much of the acreage had been tilled and cultivated, and farmhouses dotted the fertile breadbasket-like islands in an ocean. A mile to the west a cluster of buildings marked the location of the settlement, Brunstown, which Lucy had named when she was little. One day her father had returned home and told her he was starting a town to supply the needs of the loggers and asked her to come up with a name for it. She had considered everything from Brunsdale Flats to Brunsdale Haven and finally settled on the obvious.

The mansion was not constructed of wood, as Fargo had imagined it would be, but of stone and marble. The stone came from a quarry far to the north, the marble had been shipped from back East at what had to have been an astronomical expense. The result was a home that radiated wealth and power.

A mahogany door fronted the marble portico. It was opened by a butler in a neatly pressed uniform the same shade of brown as Mabel's dress. Twelve other servants were on staff, Lucy informed Fargo, including a chef from St. Louis and a stableman from Charleston. Mabel wasn't the only maid.

There were seven, all told, and given the scope of their duties, seven were barely enough.

The mansion boasted a staggering total of forty-three rooms. Each had the most expensive furnishings money could buy. In the parlor was a settee covered in tiger fur and an enormous crystal chandelier that glittered like a giant diamond. In the music room sat a grand piano and a harp that had once graced a castle in Europe. The library contained mahogany shelves ten feet high crammed with rare books. The dining room table was as long as a steamboat. In the art room hung paintings by masters from the past. Plush carpet and polished walls were the norm everywhere.

Fargo was rarely impressed by a show of great wealth, but he was impressed by what Luther Brunsdale had accomplished. In the middle of nowhere, on the edge of the frontier, the timber baron had erected a monument to the best that both civilization and culture had to offer. He couldn't imagine being able to count on one hand the number of homes like this in the entire United States.

"So what do you think'?" Lucy asked as she concluded the private tour she had given him, back in the parlor where it began.

"Your father should change his name to Midas," Fargo said, adjusting the saddlebags slung over his left shoulder. In his right hand was the Henry.

Lucy laughed, revealing those pearly white teeth of hers. "He didn't do all this to show off, you know. His philosophy is to never settle for less than the best. And why not? He can afford it." She gazed at a marvelous jade vase on an ivory stand. "My father likes to surround himself with beauty."

"Good thing he had you for a daughter, then,"

Lucy lit up like a bonfire. "What an incredibly sweet compliment. You are such a dear." Pressing against him, she kissed him lightly full on the mouth. It was short and seemingly innocent, yet she contrived to run the tip of her tongue across his upper lip and rub her bosom across his chest as she turned toward the hallway. "Come. I'll show you to your room."

Much to Fargo's disappointment, the ride down from the line camp had been too rushed for them to have much time together. Luther Brunsdale insisted on nearly riding his mount into the ground in order to arrive home with plenty of time to prepare for his business partners. Brunsdale was clearly worried, which led Fargo to suspect there was more to the visit than the recent trouble with the Phantoms. Once they had arrived, Brunsdale excused himself, committing Fargo to his daughter's keeping.

"I hope you won't mind," Luther had apologized as he hurried off with his personal secretary, Cleve Sneldon. "But I want everything to be just right for Uncle Walter and Addison Sykes."

Fargo didn't mind at all. It gave him a chance to be with the blonde, to learn whether her hand on his thigh the other night had been an invitation or a playful tease. As they climbed the spiral staircase, he admired the alluring sway of her hourglass hips and her pert, firm buttocks. A shaft of sunlight from a nearby window played over her hair, accenting the glorious golden sheen,

"My father must not be thinking straight," Lucy commented, and giggled girlishly.

"Why do you say that?"

"Ordinarily he would never let me alone with a handsome devil like you." Lucy glanced back. "Or maybe he assumes you're too noble and trustworthy to trifle with his darling little princess."

"No one has ever accused me of being noble," Fargo said.

"You can't possibly know how happy I am to hear that," Lucy declared. "But how trustworthy are you?"

"Trust is important. When a man gives his word, he should always do his best to keep it."

"Ah. Then I need to ask. Did my father make you promise not to ravish me if given half the chance?"

"No."

Lucy's cherry lips quirked upward. "His oversight might be my gain." They came to a landing and Lucy paused to reach out and trace the outline of his chin. In a whisper she said, "My father would be shocked to discover I'm not quite the paragon of daughterly virtue he believes me to be."

"You're not?"

"Hell, no. I'm a grown woman, with a grown woman's appetites. I've had a dalliance or two in my time."

"Was Rem Dinsmore one of them?" Fargo inquired.

"How in the world did you know?" Regret etched Lucy's features. "It was a mistake. I was bored and he was always fawning over me, so one afternoon up at the line camp we went for a ride and I let him have his way. As a foreman he's first-rate, but as a lover he leaves a lot to be desired."

"That's all there was to it? The one time?"

"Yes, and he's been insufferable ever since. Rem was actually naive enough to think I loved him. That I had somehow committed myself to him, and from then on I would be his and his alone. I've tried to explain, but he hovers over me like a hawk, scaring off every man who so much as says howdy." Lucy chuckled. "Except you. And now he's miles away and I have you all to myself "

"How's your head?" Fargo asked. At her father's insistence she was wearing a narrow bandage. Twice on the way down from the high country Mabel had given her teaspoons of laudanum.

"Never you mind about my scratch," Lucy said. "My head is fine. I've stopped using that awful tincture although Mabel keeps trying to get me to take more. I told her it makes me woozy and sluggish."

They walked down a carpeted hall past a number of closed doors. Halting at one, Lucy opened it and motioned for him to precede her. "Gentlemen first. This is your bedroom. I trust you'll find the accommodations satisfactory."

The best room in the best hotel in the country could not have been more so. Twice the size of a typical hotel room, it contained a canopy bed, a chest of drawers, a table and chairs, and a large window overlooking the Willamette Valley.

Fargo made a circuit, depositing his saddlebags and rifle in a corner, then moved to the window. "I have no complaints." He heard the door shut, heard a bolt being worked, and turned.

Lucy Brunsdale had a carnal gleam in her eyes as she sauntered toward him with her hands clasped behind her back and her chest arched. "My father and the entire staff will be tied up for hours. So you're all mine. Can you think of anything you would like to do to pass the time?"

"We could pay the settlement a visit," Fargo said with a straight face.

Lucy pretended to be appropriately offended. "You would rather visit a general store than enjoy my company?"

"I need some new socks," Fargo said, opening his arms so she could step into them. They stood chest to breast, her warm breath fluttering on his cheek.

"If I believed you were the least bit serious, I'd give you a sock," Lucy teased. "Right on that handsome jaw of yours."

"What do you have in mind?" Fargo asked.

"As if you don't know," was Lucy's reply, right before she molded her hungry mouth to his.

Fargo felt her silken tongue glide between his parted lips to swirl in an erotic dance with his own. She tasted delicious, as if she had just eaten strawberries, and he sucked on her tongue as he would on hard honey.

"Mmmmm," Lucy husked when she drew back. "That was nice, real nice. I knew you wouldn't bore me to death."

"There's more to come."

A seductive grin curled her luscious mouth. "Show me what you've got, big man. Don't hold back just because I'm a lady."

Fargo swooped a hand to her right breast and squeezed hard. Lucy squirmed and cooed, her eyes growing hooded as he tweaked her nipple between a thumb and forefinger through the soft fabric of her dress. His other hand slid around behind her to cup her firm posterior. She wriggled closer and kissed him again, her passion mounting.

It occurred to Fargo they should move away from the window or someone was liable to spot them. He started to sidle toward the canopy bed, glancing out the corner of his eye at the yard below. Sure enough, someone *was* watching. Mabel was outside, staring directly up at the room. Coincidence? Fargo wondered. Or was she spying on them?

Lucy pushed back. "Is something wrong? You tensed up on me."

"Everything is fine," Fargo fibbed, moving her to the side of the bed and easing her down on the quilt so they sat face-to-face. He would deal with the maid later. For now, Lucy required his full attention. Inhaling the musky scent of her perfume, he clamped his lips to hers.

They kissed and kissed, Fargo savoring the velvet sensation. Their hands explored one another with increasing abandon. He massaged both her breasts and stroked her thighs, eliciting gasps and a throaty moan. For her part, Lucy made bold to run her fingers along his leg to the growing bulge in his buckskin pants.

"Mercy me. Did you know there's a redwood growing down there?"

Fargo lowered her onto her back and began prying at the buttons and stays that would liberate her charms. It required some doing. Her dress had them front and back, but at length he peeled it from her shoulders and slid it down over her long legs. He dropped it on the floor. One by one her undergarments were added to the pile, until she was totally, breathtakingly naked, her voluptuous body bared to his feasting gaze.

"Like what you see, big man?"

That was putting it mildly. Lucy's flaxen tresses spilled over her slender shoulders almost to the swell of her up-turned mounds. Her rosy nipples were erect like twin nails, her breasts swollen like ripe melons. Below them her smooth, flat stomach descended to a golden thatch at the junction of exquisite thighs. Her right leg was crooked, her knee bent. All in all, she was as gorgeous a woman as he had ever laid eyes on.

"Admiring the scenery?"

Fargo slowly lowered his mouth to her left breast and sucked on a nipple. Lucy languidly arched her back, removed his hat, and entwined her fingers in his thick hair. He lathered first one mound and then the other, running his tongue around and around. His hands caressed her legs, up and down, up and down, never quite brushing against her core.

Lucy began to pant. Her fingernails bit into his shoulders, then traced a path down his back to his shoulder blades. Her tongue moistened his ear and she sucked on the lobe. When she tugged at his shirt, Fargo rose up and did the honors himself. He also unbuckled his gunbelt and set it on the bed beside them. His boots and pants were next.

"Oh, my," Lucy breathed with the starved look of a person who had gone without food for days on end. "All those muscles! And I wasn't kidding about your redwood, was I?" She reached out.

Fargo let her pull him to her. A moist sensation enveloped his manhood. Now it was *his* fingers that were in *her* hair, and before long he was the one who was panting. She knew just what to do to send shivers of delight up his spine. When the pleasure became so intolerable he was about to explode, Fargo pried her off and lay beside her. He kissed her eyebrows, her cheeks, her chin. He kissed the soft contours of her neck and shoulders. He circled her globes with his tongue and licked down across her belly.

Lucy gasped, her hips rising and falling rhythmically in anticipation. As his right hand roamed over her thigh and down between her legs, she opened them wide.

Fargo brushed a forefinger across her moist slit and Lucy quivered, her nails digging into his flesh. He found her swollen nether knob and gently rubbed it. At the contact Lucy closed her eyes and groaned. She was wet down there, wet and hot for him, her womanhood an inferno of smoldering desire.

Fargo inserted the tip of a finger, but only the tip, to tantalize her. Suddenly Lucy scooted her bottom downward and his finger was buried in her to the knuckle, her slick inner walls contracting around it.

"Oh! Oh! Yes!"

Fargo added a second finger, her womanhood rippling as he slowly pumped them in and out. Her hips matched his tempo, and she would shudder every now and then from the intensity of the bliss he provoked.

"Don't stop," Lucy whispered. "I want more. Lots more."

And she would get her wish, Fargo reflected with keen relish. For long minutes that blurred into one another he devoted himself to her heaving breasts while continuing to stoke her inner flames. Her body temperature, and her ardor, climbed. She writhed and moaned, her hands always in motion, doing her utmost to arouse him as he was arousing her.

Eventually Fargo withdrew his fingers and rose onto his knees between her thighs. He started to align his pole with her tunnel, but she brushed his hand aside and grabbed hold of him herself. Quaking in sensual delirium, she fed his manhood up into her innermost recess.

"Ohhhhhhhh. Yesssssssssssssssss."

Fargo grit his teeth to keep from prematurely exploding as her legs rose to wrap around his hips, her ankles locking against the small of his back.

Lucy looked up at him, her face lit by a soft smile. "This is the moment I like best."

Placing his hands on her hips, Fargo commenced to rock on his knees, driving himself up into her again and again. He went slowly to begin, gradually building in speed and force as they surged toward the pinnacle.

Lucy's burning lips were all over his neck, his shoulders, his chest. Her arms were wrapped around his torso and she clung to him as if she were drowning and he was her sole salvation. Her bottom rose to meet his thrusts with matching thrusts of her own. "Harder!" she begged. "Do it harder!"

Fargo willingly obliged, ramming up into her with vigor, and when he did, Lucy threw her head back and a soundless scream was torn from her mouth, a scream of release as she spurted. Not quite ready to do the same, Fargo paced himself, taking as long as he could, extending their mutual rapture.

Lucy's eyes snapped open and she gave him a peculiar look. "Again?" she said, more to herself than to him, a second before her body exploded in another shattering release more violent than the first.

On the brink of the abyss, it was all Fargo could do not to imitate her. Somehow he held out. Somehow he kept going. His senses reeled, though, and he could hardly focus. Lucy was fused to him, their two bodies as one, her nails churning his sides to ribbons. Her hands strayed to his backside. Under them the bed bounced wildly, but it made little noise.

"Ahh! What you do to me!" Lucy mewed.

Fargo shared her sentiments. A second later the eruption took place. His throat constricted and the bedroom spun as he gushed like a geyser. Over and over he slammed into her, nearly lifting her into the air. Pure pleasure coursed through his veins as the rest of the world receded into a haze. There was just the two of them and nothing else.

Bit by bit the room came into focus again. Fargo saw Lucy limp under him, completely spent, her throat fluttering, her breasts resplendent. He sank onto them, pillowing his cheek, as his own body sagged. For long moments they were still except for their breathing and the patter of her heart in his ear. When she shifted, Fargo eased off onto the bed, onto his side, his chin on her shoulder.

"You were magnificent," Lucy said quietly. "Thank you."

"Any time," Fargo said, resisting the nip of fatigue. He hadn't had much sleep the night before. They had ridden until almost midnight, then been on the go again at first light, arriving at the mansion an hour after sunrise. The Ovaro was tucked in the stable, and Skye's time was his own until evening when he was invited to another supper. The Syndicate members, Walter and Addison, were not due for another day or so.

Lucy tittered. "My father would have a conniption if he found out. He thinks proper young ladies should save themselves for wedlock."

An object was gouging Fargo in the back. Groping behind himself, he moved his gunbelt.

"I've tried to explain how I feel, but he doesn't care to hear it," Lucy elaborated. "He says only hussies sleep with men for the fun of it. I'm no hussy. But I'm not a nun, either." Shifting, she draped an arm across him. "When I finally tie the knot, I'll be true to the man I love. Until then, well . . ." She shrugged. "Can I help it if I like sex now and again?"

"What about Mabel?" Fargo asked.

Lucy stared at him. "Why? Are you interested? Well, you can forget it. She hasn't so much as looked twice at a man the whole time she's been with us. The cook showed some interest in her a while ago but she put him in his place. She never even talks about men like the other maids do."

"How is it your father never remarried?"

"He loved my mother, is why. She was the only one for him. And since she passed on, he's been married to the timber business. He works twelve, fourteen hours a day. It doesn't leave much time for socializing."

Fargo rolled onto his back. He had to get up, had to do something, or he would fall asleep. Loud voices outside galvanized him into rising and padding to the right of the window so he could peer out without being seen.

A heavy red coach pulled by six magnificent black horses was winding up the gravel lane toward the mansion. The horses were caked with sweat and dust from a long journey. Dust also layered the coach, a splendid newer model with glistening brass rails that bordered the luggage rack and the driver's box, brass oil lamps, and hickory and ash running gear. Basswood panels covered the sides. Large trunks were tied in place on the rack while others jutted against the leather cover over the rear boot.

The driver wore an immaculate black outfit and derby hat, and wielded a long whip with dexterous skill. All four of the leather curtains over the windows had been rolled up to admit air. Three men were inside, two on the front seat, one at the rear. Painted in bright-yellow letters on the doors were the words BRUNSDALE TIMBER SYNDICATE.

"Who is it?" Lucy asked sleepily. "It can't be Doc Stephens. He sent word he can't get here until tomorrow. Agatha Cooper is about to have a baby."

Fargo described the coach. The blonde immediately shot off the canopy bed as if fired from a catapult and dashed to the sill.

"Good God! Not them! Not yet!"

"Walter Brunsdale and Addison Sykes?" Fargo deduced.

"One other. I don't know who the third man is." Lucy ran to her clothes and commenced pulling them on as if she were in a race to see who could get dressed first. "I need to go. My father will want me with him when he meets them."

"Want me to tag along?" Fargo offered.

"No. I'll see you later. At supper if not sooner." Lucy's fingers were flying. "In case my father hasn't filled you in, relations with the other two have soured in recent years. Particularly between my father and Addison Sykes. Sykes has an exalted notion of himself and overrates his importance to the Syndicate."

"How does your great-uncle fit in?"

Lucy sneered. "Ever seen a trained dog jump through hoops? Uncle Walter would walk across a bed of burning coals if Addison Sykes told him to. He has as much gumption as a bowl of mush."

In under a minute she was dressed and gone, pecking Fargo on the cheek on her way out. "Find something to keep you busy until supper."

Fargo sat on the edge of the bed and pulled on his buckskins and boots, then strapped on his gunbelt and donned his bandanna and hat. When he mentioned visiting the settlement earlier, he had been serious. And there was no time like the present.

Leaving the room, Fargo took a couple of steps, only to halt when someone to his rear cleared their throat.

"Hold on there, sir. These are for you."

Pivoting, Fargo saw Mabel strolling toward him with a pitcher of water and a couple of towels. The brunette was smiling, but the smile never touched her dark eyes. "You sure get around," he said. "I thought I saw you outside a while ago."

"A maid's work is never done, sir," Mabel said. "Between the master of the house and Miss Brunsdale, I'm kept hopping from dawn until bedtime." She nodded at the door. "Do you mind if I put these inside?"

"Be my guest." Fargo opened it for her and she crossed to the night stand and set them down. Her loose-fitting uniform made it difficult to tell much about her body, but from her lithe movements and the manner in which her bosom jiggled when she straightened, Fargo was willing to bet she was almost as finely formed as Lucy. "Do you like working for the Brunsdales?"

"They pay extremely well, sir," Mabel said matter-of-factly. "But I'm glad I only agreed to hire on for a year. It's a little too isolated out here for my tastes. When my contract is up, I plan to head for New Orleans. I have relatives there who will put me up while I search for a new job."

"You shouldn't have any trouble finding one with Luther Brunsdale as a reference," Fargo mentioned.

Mabel came out into the hall, started to leave, then hesitated. "If I may be so bold, perhaps you and I can get together before you head back up into the mountains. I'd like to hear about all the adventures Mr. Brunsdale says you've had."

"You would?" Fargo could not have been more taken aback if she had stripped naked and danced a jig.

"Absolutely. I hope you'll take me up on it. I have a free hour to myself every evening from nine until ten." Mabel leaned toward him and rubbed her hand across his cheek. "You won't regret it, I assure you. When I let my hair down, I can be as frisky as the next woman." Winking, she ambled down the hall.

Most men would be undeniably flattered, but Fargo was left puzzling over a question he voiced aloud to himself. "What the hell was that all about?"

The walls had no answer.

6

Just outside the settlement a small but neatly painted sign bore the name BRUNSTOWN. Underneath, in smaller print, was the boast POPULATION 33 AND GROWING.

A single rutted street was flanked by over a dozen buildings on either side. In addition to the general store, feed store, and loggers' emporium, there was a millinery for women, a combination barber and tool sharpening shop, an establishment that billed itself as ABIGAIL'S EATERY, a blacksmith's, and others. At either end of town stood quaint frame houses bordered by white picket fences.

Fargo was halfway down the street when it struck him something was missing, something almost every settlement and town had. There were no saloons, no taverns, no establishment at all where hard liquor was served or gambling was indulged. Brunstown immediately leaped to the top of his list of places he wouldn't visit twice if he could help it.

People bustled industriously about. Timbermen with time off were buying new clothes and whatever equipment they needed. Farmers in from the fields with their wives and families were going from store to store.

Since the hitch rails in front of the general store and the Brunsdale Syndicate Emporium were full, Fargo drew rein at the hitch rail in front of the feed store. A buckboard parked to one side was being loaded by a big-boned farmer in homespun, and another farmer was in earnest debate with a clerk.

Dismounting, Fargo stretched and stepped up onto the

boardwalk. He touched his hat brim to a pair of women in bonnets and long dresses, but neither looked him in the eye. He wasn't offended. Both wore wedding rings, and as a general rule married women avoided contact with men they didn't know, which was fine by Fargo. He would rather tangle with a rifled grizzly than face the wrath of a jealous husband.

Fargo needed information, and the best place to start, he figured, was Ely's General Store. In frontier communities, the general store was where everyone went for the latest news and gossip. This one was no different. Half a dozen farmers were seated by the cracker barrel, jawing. Women were at a counter paging through the latest catalogs, and off to the right a gray-haired matron was inspecting bolts of yard goods.

A balding man in his forties, a white apron around his ample waist, bestowed a friendly smile as Fargo came up the center aisle. "Morning, friend. Or should I say good afternoon? Ely Johnson at your service. What can I do for you?"

Fargo was conscious of being stared at by practically everyone. Frontiersmen were a rare sight in Brunstown. "I need some socks."

"Right this way." Ely moved around the counter, past the dry goods, and over to the clothing section. "I have some of the best woolen socks being sold today. They don't shrink much when wet and they'll keep your feet warm in the coldest of weather." Without trying to seem too nosy, he glanced at Fargo and said, "Passing through, are you?"

"I'm staying at the Brunsdales'," Fargo mentioned.

All conversation in the store ceased. Ely Johnson looked as if he had swallowed a cactus. "At the big house? With Mr. Brunsdale himself?"

"Luther hired me to track down the Phantoms."

Ely scooped up an armful of socks, and shoved them at him. "Here. Take as many as you want. No charge. If you can put an end to the attacks, you'll be doing our town a great favor."

"I'm willing to pay," Fargo said.

"Keep your money. Just stop the damn Indians. They've brought the logging to a halt, and sales have suffered because of it. It's gotten so bad, the loggers aren't sure if they'll have jobs by the end of the month."

Fargo chose a pair, and while examining them he asked, "Get many Indians in here?"

"In town? Oh, a few Calapooyans from time to time, but they're as peaceable as can be. A lot of them are taking up white ways and they're quite civilized."

"No others?" Fargo asked, choosing another pair. "I hear there are some Modocs in the valley."

Ely shook his head. "Who told you that? There's just one that I know of. Modoc Jim. Rem Dinsmore brought him in to help stop the raids. Not that it's done any good." Ely paused. "Modoc Jim has been in my store a few times. He's not very talkative, but he always buys enough flour and coffee and whatnot to outfit an army."

"You don't say." Fargo wagged the pair of socks and reached into a pocket. "I'd still like to pay you."

"Forget it. And if there's anything else you want, you only have to ask."

"I'm obliged," Fargo said. He started for the door. "I almost forgot. Have you seen any strangers in town the past few months?"

"Sure haven't," Ely responded. "Unless you count the three uppity roosters who went through here this morning in a fancy coach. They wouldn't say who they were or why they were here, although one of them mentioned some big changes were in store for the Syndicate."

"Again, thanks." As Fargo walked past the cracker box, an elderly man puffing on a pipe snagged his sleeve.

"Pardon me, mister. I couldn't help overhearing. My name is Tyler, and I have a farm ten miles south of town, close to the mountains."

"What can I do for you?"

"You mentioned strangers," Tyler said. "Sometime back, four or five months, I reckon it was, my wife looked out the window one night and saw a light off yonder. I saddled up my mule and went for a look-see. It was a campfire, with five men around it. I tried to come up on them quiet-like to ask what they were doing on my property, but they must have heard me because they lit out of there as if their backsides were on fire. I never did get a good look at them."

"They threw their saddles on their horses that quick?"

"Land's sakes, no. Their horses were already saddled. I reckon they hadn't got around to bedding down for the night yet."

Fargo had more than ever to mull over as he stepped out into the bright sunlight. He put the socks in his saddlebags, then crossed the street to the Brunsdale Syndicate Emporium. As he stepped onto the boardwalk, three loggers lounging at the corner of the building caught sight of him and nudged one another.

Only a few timbermen were inside. The aisles were lined with tools of their trade, everything from axes to wedges to peavey heads. A middle-aged man with bushy sideburns and an oiled mustache was stacking crates, and Fargo went over. "Are you the owner?"

"Ira Pearson, the manager," the man said without glancing up. "I run the store for the Syndicate. What can I do for you?"

"A coach came through town a while ago. Did the men inside it pay you a visit?"

Pearson stopped stacking. "One did. A big fella waltzed in here as if he owned the place and badgered me with a lot of damn fool questions. I told him to take it up with Mr. Brunsdale." Pearson's eyes narrowed. "Why? What is it to you?"

"Just curious. Did this hombre tell you who he was?"

"No. And I didn't ask. Him and his snotty ways." Pearson swore under his breath. "He had the gall to tell me he didn't think the Syndicate was getting its money's worth out of the emporium. That were it up to him, he could increase the profits another ten percent."

"Did he ask to look at your books?"

Pearson's eyes narrowed even more. "How did you know? Yes, he did, but my ledgers are my business. I told him in no uncertain terms that the only other person who has access to them is Luther Brunsdale himself, or Brunsdale's secretary, Cleve Sneldon."

"What did the man do?"

"He laughed and left. Just like that. I looked out the window and saw the coach go riding off toward the Brunsdale place." Pearson stopped. "Do you know who they were?"

The manager had been helpful so Fargo repaid the courtesy. "Addison Sykes and Walter Brunsdale, the other two partners in the Syndicate."

"You don't say? What in the world are they doing here? Near as I know, they like to sit off in Ohio and rake in the money Mr. Brunsdale earns."

"The people here think highly of Luther, don't they?"

"Mister, he's the salt of the earth. He always treats his workers decently, always gives the other fellow a fair shake. He cares about people. Why, he brought in Doc Stephens and supplements Doc's earnings out of the company payroll just so we'll have our own sawbones. Ask around. Not one person in town has a bad thing to say about him."

Fargo thanked Pearson and walked back out. He was learning a lot but still wasn't quite sure how it all fit together. He had about concluded the Phantoms weren't an unknown tribe. All the facts hinted otherwise. If they weren't, then they had to be led by someone who was uncommonly skilled at woodlore, and the only person he had met who fit the bill was Modoc Jim. But he could think of no reason for the Modoc to go around murdering people.

"Say there, mister."

A shadow fell across him, and Fargo shifted. The three burly timbermen who had been lounging at the corner of the building had walked over while he was deep in thought. One had a bushy red beard, and across his shoulder rested a long wooden mallet, the kind loggers used to drive wedges into sawcuts and to split shakes. The second man held a picka-roon, an axe-like tool that had a single tapered point that was driven into logs to move them. The third man carried a peavey, a five-foot pole with a wicked hook at the end.

"We have a bone to pick with you," bushy-beard said.

Fargo didn't respond.

"That we do," the man with the pickaroon said. "You've been stepping out of line and we aim to set you right."

The logger with the peavy grinned wickedly. "Cat got your tongue? Or maybe you're too scared to talk?"

"Oh, I can talk, all right," Fargo said. "I'm just waiting for you jackasses to get to the point."

Bushy-beard's cheeks turned as red as his beard. "Fair enough. Rumor has it you've been trifling where you shouldn't."

"Lucy Brunsdale is spoken for," the man with the peavey stated, "and the man who intends to marry her doesn't like how you've been spending so much time in her company."

The third logger hefted the pickaroon. "So he asked us to do him a favor and see that you climb on that pinto of yours and head elsewhere. California is real nice this time of year. Or maybe you have a hankering to go back East."

"Hell, we don't care where you go," bushy-beard said, "so long as you *go*."

"And if I refuse?" Fargo asked.

The man with the peavey chuckled. "You don't want to be that dumb. Trust us." He gave the peavey a deft twirl. "We'll pound you into the boardwalk so fast, you won't know what hit you."

"Make it easy on yourself," suggested the timberman hold-ing the pickaroon. "Turn around and march straight to your horse. We'll tag along to make sure you don't have second thoughts."

Fargo looked at each of them in turn. "I'd like to know. Did Rem Dinsmore send you down from the line camp? Or were you already here and he somehow sent word to you?"

"What difference does it make?" bushy-beard growled, and

caught himself. "Besides, no one said Rem is involved. It could be anyone."

"And I was born this morning," Fargo said. He saw that people along the street had realized something was amiss and were stopping to stare. "Take a message to Dinsmore for me. I'll leave when I'm damn good and ready. If he doesn't like it, he can tell me to my face instead of sending three dunderheads to do his dirty work."

"Dunderheads, are we?" the man with the pickaroon said, and with that, he swung the pickaroon in an overhand arc. Were it to connect, the metal tip would embed itself in Fargo's skull, but Fargo sidestepped and the point thudded into the boardwalk instead, splitting a plank and lodging fast. Swearing, the man tried to jerk it loose. Fargo had other ideas. He whipped his fist into the logger's jaw and sent him stumbling back against the man with the peavey.

Bushy-beard sprang to their aid. His long wooden mallet sizzled the air, streaking at Fargo's face. Ducking, Fargo drove a fist into the man's stomach, and when the redheaded logger doubled over, he delivered an uppercut that crumpled him like so much paper.

Seizing the mallet's handle, Fargo tore it from the man's grasp. He rotated as the other two pounced. The peavey lanced low, the pickaroon sheared high. Wrenching himself to the right, Fargo avoided the peavey's hook even as he blocked the pickaroon with a swing of the mallet.

Up and down the dusty street, people were yelling and rushing to witness the clash. Someone bawled for them to stop fighting, but the loggers ignored him and came at Fargo again.

The man with the pickaroon pumped his arms from side to side, seeking to batter down Fargo's guard by sheer brute strength. Against a weaker adversary it might have worked. But Fargo was as strong if not stronger, and it was the man with the pickaroon who found himself on the defensive. Fargo flailed furiously at him with the heavy mallet. The logger

72

was driven back against the Emporium, tripped over a display of climbing irons, and fell.

Spinning, Fargo parried another thrust of the peavey. Not to be denied, the timberman speared it at his throat. Again Fargo countered, only this time the peavey's hook caught on the mallet's handle and they became locked together. Fargo tugged, in vain. The logger was doing likewise, straining so hard the veins in his temples bulged. Suddenly letting go, Fargo punched the man in the face, throwing his entire body into it.

Now two were down, but the logger with the pickaroon had regained his feet and waded in like a Viking berserker, raining blows right and left. Fargo had to fling himself backward to save himself. The metal tip flashed before his eyes, almost clipping his nose. It whisked past his cheek, brushing his buckskin shirt. He had to do something, and he had do it soon, or one of the blows was bound to connect.

Fargo's hand dropped to his Colt. No one could blame him for shooting. It was a clear-cut case of self-defense if ever there was, one. But as he drew, the logger blundered onto the split plank and his boot sank into the gap, bringing him to a halt.

The man desperately levered his leg upward, but his foot was stuck. Inadvertently, he let the pickaroon drop.

Fargo smashed the Colt's barrel against the logger's jaw, then stood over the three unconscious forms waiting for one to stir.

Onlookers gathered around, whispering among themselves. No one made bold to interfere.

"Excuse me, folks! Please let me through!"

The crowd parted to permit Ely Johnson access to the boardwalk. He made a clucking noise as he surveyed Fargo's handiwork. "I saw the whole thing from my store window. What was this all about, mister? Why did they attack you?"

"It's personal," Fargo said.

Johnson wiped his hands on his apron. "It wouldn't have anything to do with Cleve Sneldon's visit this morning, would it? I saw him talking to these three out by my store, and when I went over, they clammed up as if I'd caught them with their hands in a jar of hard candy."

Fargo no longer needed to stay. He had the answer to the question he was going to ask the trio. "When they come to, tell them the Willamette Valley is bad for their health. Tell them they should look for work elsewhere." He stalked toward the feed store, the people nearly falling over themselves to get out of his way.

Once on the Ovaro, Fargo held to a walk. He toyed with the notion of visiting the sawmill, located a mile north of the mansion, but decided it would serve no purpose. So he headed back, in no great hurry, not when he had so much to consider. Rem Dinsmore, for starters. The bull of the woods, as camp foremen were called, had let his jealousy swamp his common sense and had gone too far. There would be a reckoning, Fargo promised himself, and it would not be to Dinsmore's liking.

As for the Phantoms, they were as big a mystery as ever. Because if they truly weren't Indians, then *who were they?* And what did they hope to accomplish by crippling the Brunsdale Timber Syndicate? Practically every business in the settlement depended on it to stay afloat.

And now, on top of everything else, Walter Brunsdale and Addison Sykes had arrived to take advantage of the situation. As if Luther did not have enough headaches.

Fargo thought about the farmer at the general store, the one who caught riders camped on his property. Was it a coincidence or did it have a bearing on the attacks?

In due course the mansion came into sight, towering amid stately oaks and weeping willows. Beyond reared the mountains, and as Fargo gazed at them, he spied a bright gleam of light, much like the one off the Phantom's rifle barrel the other day at the line camp. It was miles up, on a ridge bare of timber. As Fargo watched, the gleam was repeated, not once but several times, and he realized it was deliberate.

Someone was up there with a mirror, signaling. But signaling whom? Where?

Fargo twisted in the saddle, but saw no answering gleam in the direction of the settlement. When he turned around, though, he glimpsed a brief shimmering glow from the vicinity of the mansion.

A tap of his spurs brought the Ovaro to a gallop, and Fargo raced the final quarter-mile. Veering toward the rear of the stable, where he was certain the person responsible had been, he searched among the trees. No one was there.

The stableman was currying a mare when Fargo trotted around to the front. "Will you take care of my horse for me?"

"Gladly, sir. That's why I'm here,"

"Did you see anyone off in the trees a minute ago?" Fargo asked. "Or walking toward the house?"

"No, sir, I surely didn't. But I've been busy. I haven't paid much attention to what's been going on around me. Sorry."

Peeved fate had thwarted him, Fargo swung down and walked toward the mansion, taking the Henry and his saddlebags. He had gone over halfway when he saw Mabel approaching in great haste.

"Mr. Fargo! I can use your help," the brunette said urgently. "I was at an upstairs window a couple of minutes ago and swore I saw several bright flashes from out here somewhere. I mentioned them to Miss Brunsdale and she sent me to investigate."

"I saw them too, but I couldn't find who did it," Fargo disclosed. He said nothing about the flashes up on the mountain. He still didn't trust her any farther than he could lift the mansion.

"What do you think it was?"

"It's hard to say," Fargo said.

Stopping, Mabel fell into step next to him as he tramped by. "I suppose I should get on with my duties, then. The whole staff is in an uproar. Mr. Brunsdale is hosting a special meal tonight for his guests from Ohio, and he's invited a lot of prominent people from the settlement."

"I guess us getting together tonight is out," Fargo remarked.

"Afraid so," Mabel said, and rubbed the back of her hand across the back of his. "But there's always tomorrow night. If you're still around, that is."

"Where else would I be?"

Mabel fussed with the bun in her hair. "Back up in the mountains. I happened to hear Mr. Brunsdale say you were going back up soon to track down the Phantoms." She smiled. "More's the pity. I'm looking forward to having you all to myself. " Her hand brushed his a second time.

Fargo doubted she was sincere. He couldn't shake the feeling she was up to no good, and the sight of a high hedge ahead gave him an idea how he could put her to the test. When they reached it he suddenly grabbed her and pulled her into its shadow where no one was likely to see them. Bending, he fused his mouth to hers and ran his hands down over the back of her uniform to her bottom. He figured she would resist, perhaps even slap him, but to his considerable consternation, her arms looped up around his neck and she pulled him hard against her soft body. Her lips parted, her tongue darting out to stroke his. Their kiss lingered on and on. He was the one who broke it, not her.

"My, my, you can definitely make a girl's head spin," Mabel said huskily, not lowering her arms. "I thought as much after Miss Brunsdale raved about you so."

"She did?" Fargo said, his doubts eroding from under him. "She told me you don't like men."

Mabel's laugh tinkled on the breeze. "I can see where she would get that impression. But it's not as if I have the cream of the crop to choose from. Loggers are a little too unkempt and ill-mannered for my tastes, and no one else on the staff remotely interests me." She kissed his chin. "Perhaps I'm too particular, but I don't hop into bed with a man unless he makes me feel all warm inside. Like you do."

Fargo felt like a fool. "I saw you out the window this morning, watching us."

"You did? I had just got done stringing clothes on the line

and was on my way back in. I must say, I needed a cold bath after seeing the two of you together."

"I thought maybe you were spying on us. The other day at the line camp I saw you eavesdropping when Lucy was talking to me."

Mabel cocked her head quizzically. "How could you think such a thing? I simply didn't want to intrude on your conversation. A good servant knows when to be seen and not heard, but an outstanding servant knows when not to be seen at all." She grinned, and her eyes lit with genuine amusement. "You don't know much about servants, do you?"

Fargo had a ridiculous urge to beat his head against the nearest tree. "We should be careful. Lucy might not like us being together, and I wouldn't want to cost you your job." Stepping from the shadows, he steered her up the footpath.

"You needn't worry on that account," Mabel said. "Miss Brunsdale has the morals of a she-goat. She sleeps with every man she can, then casts them aside like spoiled leftovers." Mabel glanced at him. "A word to the wise."

"Any other secrets about the Brunsdales you care to share?" Fargo prompted. It was just possible she could help him unravel some of the secrets shrouding the Syndicate and the Phantoms.

"And violate their trust?" Mabel said. "The cardinal rule of being a servant is that we never, ever betray a confidence, or impart information we overhear." She gazed toward the mansion. "But I will tell you strange intrigues are taking place. No one is quite how they seem to be."

"Does that include Rem Dinsmore?"

"Him most of all. He sneaks around spying on Miss Brunsdale all the time, and has any man who so much as looks at her beat up. He's also quite close to Cleve Sneldon, although what the two have in common eludes me."

Fargo's growing trust in her climbed several rungs. Based on the storekeeper's account, he was positive it had been Sneldon who relayed a message from Dinsmore to the three loggers in the settlement. "If you won't talk about the Brunsdales, how about the Phantoms? Anything you know that I don't?"

"Only that about five weeks ago a severed finger from one of the dead loggers was found lying next to Mr. Brunsdale's bed at the line camp. He woke up and there it was. Scared him something awful. It's why he sent for you."

Fargo was dumfounded. No earthly reason existed for a warrior to have done such a thing. After going to all the trouble of sneaking into the line camp, into Brunsdale's very bedroom, it made more sense for the intruder to kill him, not leave a grisly memento. It was added proof, as if any more were needed, the Phantoms weren't Indians. "Thanks, Mabel. Say, I never caught your last name."

"Easy."

"What is?"

"My name, silly. Mabel Easy." The brunette winked at him. "Play your cards right and you just might find out if it's true."

7

The scene was familiar but the setting was different.

In a dining room opulent enough for a sultan, Skye Fargo gazed the length of the long mahogany table and watched as servant after servant added a new dish to the feast. There were four kinds of soup including clam chowder, a favorite of his that was hard to come by on the frontier since only the very finest of restaurants served it. There was wheat bread, rye bread, white bread, and freshly baked rolls still warm from the oven. Platters were heaped high with venison, elk meat, beef, lamb, duck, and rabbit. Potatoes in every form and a host of vegetables were put out for those who wanted them. Dumplings, puddings, curries, and more were liberally spread out.

For Fargo, it wasn't a matter of what to eat so much as what *not* to eat. All he had to do was point at a dish and a servant added a portion to his plate. Mabel was waiting on him personally. From her prim, efficient behavior, none of the other guests would ever guess she knew him, let alone had shared an intimate interlude with him.

Fourteen people were seated around the table, which was barely a third of the number of seats available. At the head sat Luther Brunsdale. Lucy was on his right, Cleve Sneldon next to her, then Doc Stephens, Ely Johnson, Ira Pearson, the owner of the feed store, and Fargo. On Luther's left were Walter Brunsdale; Addison Sykes; the weasel of a man who had arrived with them, Reginald Sumersby; and several other business owners from Brunstown.

Instead of laughing and joking and having a grand time, everyone was subdued and rarely spoke unless spoken to. Fargo suspected that word of the rift between Luther and his two partners had spread throughout the settlement, and no one knew quite what to expect. That they all liked and admired Luther made the strain on their nerves worse.

Luther got things rolling with a toast. Rising with a crystal glass in hand, he said, "Friends and associates, I thank you for attending. Eat hearty and enjoy yourselves. Afterward, it's my understanding my uncle has an announcement to make that concerns all of us."

Walter Brunsdale smiled thinly. Old enough to be mistaken for Methuselah, even his wrinkles had wrinkles. His hair consisted of white wisps ringing a bald center. He had a beaked nose and virtually no chin, and when he talked, his voice cracked as if his vocal chords were about worn out. It was a wonder he had survived the journey from Ohio.

In contrast, Addison Sykes radiated vitality and strength much like the sun radiated heat and light. He was a huge man, taller than Fargo and broader of shoulder and girth, and with a much bigger belly. He had a broad, florid face dominated by bushy eyebrows and an unseemly thick mouth and jowls. His custom-made suit glistened with gold buttons, and he wore a cravat with a gold stickpin.

Reginald Sumersby was short, thin, and shifty, with beady eyes and a sour disposition. Fargo had taken an immediate dislike to him. Sumersby was a lawyer, and he always hovered in Sykes's shadow.

Small talk was made. The merchants told how business had dropped off because of the Phantoms, and everyone complained because the Army had been unable to quell the uprising. Captain Barker was due to arrive in the area within a few days, and most scoffed at Ely Johnson when he commented that maybe this time Barker would run the Indians to ground.

Fargo was treating himself to chocolate pudding when his name was mentioned.

"Perhaps you would be so kind as to share what you have learned about the Phantoms for the benefit of my partners," Luther Brunsdale said. "They don't seem to understand the magnitude of the problem."

"There is more to it than meets the eye," Fargo said. He was not yet ready to let everyone know he believed the Phantoms weren't Indians. He needed more proof or they would laugh him to scorn.

Addison Sykes stopped chomping on a slab of elk meat long enough to say in his booming bass voice, "I find it hard to believe one of the best scouts on the continent can't track down a few paltry savages."

Fargo restrained his temper and responded, "I only arrived a few days ago. But I can tell you the Phantoms aren't run-of-the-mill Indians. You can't blame Luther for not being able to stop their raids."

"Let us be the judge of what we can and can't do," Addison responded gruffly. "There is more involved here than you realize."

"I realize more than you think," Fargo countered, staring the man-mountain right in the eyes.

Addison never batted an eyelid, but Walter Brunsdale started and glanced up sharply. "What does that mean, young man?"

Addison Sykes waved a thick hand. "It means nothing, Walter. Vagueness is the last resort of incompetence. Mr. Fargo can't find the savages so he's trying to convince us they must be exceptional in some respect."

"They are exceptional," Luther said. "It's been months since the attacks began and no one has ever set eyes on them and lived."

"So?" Addison chomped a few times. "What does that prove? I've heard the Sioux and the Cheyenne, to name just a couple, are elusive in their own right. An officer we met on the way out told us that trying to hunt them down is like trying to hunt ghosts. Their warriors are will-of-the-wisps who can disappear at will."

"Then you can appreciate what I'm up against," Luther said.

Addison swallowed and set down his fork. "To be frank, your failure is vastly disappointing. These aren't Sioux we're talking about. These are a handful of woodland heathens. Yet you have let them bring the Syndicate's logging to a virtual standstill. We are losing thousands of dollars a day, and we find it intolerable."

"What do you intend to do?"

"After the meal, Luther. After the meal."

Fargo saw resentment flare in most of the townspeople. Sykes was treating Luther as if he were an underling, not an equal. He was surprised Luther let the man get away with it, but the meal resumed with hardly anyone talking until Doc Stephens made a comment.

"You'll be happy to hear, Luther, that your little girl is doing fine. Your maid knew just what to do to prevent infection. Lucy will have a small scar, but it won't detract from her beauty." Stephens was a kindly old man who had a face like a hound dog and big, owlish eyes.

"That's great to hear, Doc," Luther said warmly. "Lord knows, I can use some good news. All I receive lately is bad. Which reminds me." He looked at Fargo. "Ely and Ira Pearson tell me you had a run-in with several of my logging crew today. Who were they and what was it about?"

"It was nothing," Fargo said as all eyes swung toward him. He would personally deal with Rem Dinsmore, the man responsible, when the time came.

"That's not what I heard," Luther pressed him. "They say you were nearly killed. The men involved must be punished."

"I'll handle it," Fargo said. "It's my problem, not yours."

"I beg to differ. They are my employees. As such, they must be held to account when they step out of bounds. Based on the descriptions I was given, I think I know who two of them were. They've left the settlement, though, and I don't know where they've gone. Perhaps to the line camp. I'll confront them when we get there."

Lucy had been fiddling with a bow on her dress. Now she stopped and asked, "You're going back up? So soon?"

"I'm taking Addison and Walter there so they can see for themselves what I've been up against," Luther answered.

"Is that wise, Father? Think of the danger."

"Mr. Fargo and seven of my men will accompany us," Luther said. "We'll be perfectly safe." As an afterthought he disclosed, "We leave tomorrow morning."

"If you're going, so am I," Lucy declared. She held up a hand when he began to object. "Don't try to stop me. It won't do any good. If it's safe enough for you, it's safe enough for me. I'll take Mabel along to watch over me."

Fargo noticed that neither Addison Sykes nor Walter Brunsdale acted the least bit concerned about venturing into an area where a war party was on a supposed rampage. He could not resist saying, "It's lucky for all of us the Phantoms don't know we're coming. They could destroy the Timber Syndicate with one attack."

"I fear no man, red or white," Addison Sykes said, and turned toward Luther. "As for your situation, no problem is unsolvable. Your inability to control these simple savages is baffling and hints at a defect of character."

"Care to expand on that?" Luther said.

Walter Brunsdale placed a hand on Sykes's broad arm. "Not now. We should do him the courtesy of waiting until the others have gone."

"Why?" Addison said. "It will be common knowledge before too long. We might as well clear the air now, as it were, and let everyone know our position." He scanned those present. "I know that many of you hold Luther in the highest regard. You rightfully view him as the man who made your livelihoods possible. So I'll understand if what I am about to say angers you."

Everyone had stopped eating. Glancing to his right, Fargo saw a peculiar grin twisting Cleve Sneldon's features.

Addison rose, his massive bulk towering over the mahogany table. "As all of you are aware, the Brunsdale Timber Syndicate was formed by Luther and Walter and myself. The dream was Luther's, but most of the initial money to fund the operation was mine. It was Walter who brought the idea to my attention, and I agreed to put up the capital and let Luther run things."

"For which I have always been grateful," Luther interjected.

Addison ignored him. "Walter and I have been involved in all major decisions, but there was never any need for us to take a hand in the day-to-day operation of the enterprise. Until now."

Ely Johnson and some of the store owners swapped anxious looks.

"Before you think this is a rush to judgment on our part, you should know that for quite some time Walter and I have been unhappy with how Luther has been managing things. We have made a number of suggestions he has refused to follow, and as a result, our profits have not been as high as they should be. Now this latest development. It all adds up to a less than stellar performance, and unless Luther can convince us he's right and we're wrong, Walter and I intend to vote him out of the Syndicate and replace him with Reginald Sumersby, here, a close friend of mine."

A chill pervaded the room. Those at the table were frozen in place, but only for a few moments. Four or five of the business owners threw comments at Sykes and Walter, all of them speaking at once.

The loudest was Ely Johnson, who summed up the sentiments of the majority when he bellowed, "Of all the gall! Luther built Brunsdale Timber from the ground up. You can't just toss him out with the dirty wash water."

Addison held up a hand. "Calm yourselves! I assure you we have the best interests of the Syndicate at heart." Addison leaned forward, his hands on either side of his plate. "Bear in mind we never had to come here. We could have sent a formal notice of dismissal from Ohio, and there wasn't a damn thing Luther could do about it. But we wanted to give him a fair hearing. So we came all the way to Oregon to resolve the crisis in person."

"Or was it to have the satisfaction of firing him in person?" Lucy snapped.

"I'm not that petty," Addison said. "This is business, not personal." He paused. "What most of you don't realize is that the Brunsdale Timber Syndicate isn't the only business I've invested in over the years. I expect the same excellence from all of them,"

Luther was as rigid as a statue. "Yes, you expect to make as much money as you possibly can."

"You make it sound like a crime," Addison said. "An investor expects a reasonable return on his money."

Now Luther stood. "Tell them the rest of it. Tell them how you have been pressuring me to expand our operation. Share your grand scheme."

"Why not?" Addison said, straightening. "All of you no doubt think the Syndicate has been doing quite well. Growth has been steady. Each year we make more money than the year before. Each year we add more men to the payroll."

"Sounds good to me," Ira Pearson said.

"To small minds a small profit is always more than enough," Addison replied. "But why settle for a pittance when we can reap a fortune? Why settle for earning hundreds of thousands yearly when we can earn *millions*?"

"How do you propose to do that?" Doc Stephens inquired.

"Quite simply. By supplying timber not just to the settlers in the Willamette Valley, or the Northwest, but to much of the rest of the country, as well. By having the Brunsdale Timber Syndicate become the primary supplier of wood throughout the United States." Addison was warming to his subject. "Think of it! Other than a few logging companies in California and one north of the Columbia River, we have no serious competition. With the political clout I have, I could arrange for our Syndicate to increase in size tenfold."

"Wait a minute," one of the townsmen said. "To do that, you'd need to cut down ten times as much timber."

"A hundred times as much," Addison corrected him.

Luther spiked a finger at Sykes. "Which is exactly why I've always opposed the plan. In a decade there wouldn't be a tree left in the southern half of the state. You want to ravage the land to line your pocket. It's not right."

Addison's chest swelled. "Right or wrong doesn't enter into it. First and foremost, we are businessmen. Profit is all that counts. For over a year now I've been trying to get you to see that. I've reasoned with you. Explained the prospects again and again. But you stubbornly refuse to go along."

"And I will continue to refuse."

Addison nodded at Ely Johnson. "You there. What do you currently earn? Five thousand a year, over and above expenses? Imagine earning twenty-five thousand." He gestured at the townsmen. "All of you could do the same. So what if in ten years the timber is gone? By then everyone here will have enough money to retire in comfort. I ask you, what is wrong with that?"

One of the businessmen said in awe, "Twenty-five thousand a year? Lordy, what I wouldn't give to make that much."

Ely Johnson smacked the table. "If Luther says it's not right, that's enough for me. All of us should stick by him."

"What you do is irrelevant," Addison said. The final choice is up to Walter and myself. Once we've surveyed the scope of the operation, we will render our decision. And that, gentlemen, will be that." He sat back down and stabbed his fork into another chunk of elk meat.

Fargo had more food for thought. If his hunch was right, and the Phantoms weren't Indians, could the raids on the loggers and the power struggle taking place for control of the Syndicate be related? It wasn't as far-fetched as it sounded. But again, he needed proof before he could accuse anyone of wrongdoing.

The rest of the meal was conducted in virtual silence, Every now and then Addison Sykes commented on various dishes, but no one else had anything to say. Luther picked at his food, his appetite gone. Lucy constantly glared at Addison. Walter Brunsdale seemed a bit sad. Most of the business owners were pondering the promise of more money. And Reginald Sumersby, the heir apparent to Luther's position, sat there with a silly smirk on his face.

The servants shared the tension. They spoke in whispers when they spoke at all, and swiftly spirited empty plates and bowls out of the dining room.

Presently Luther rose to escort the physician and townsmen to the door. Lucy trailed along, leaving Fargo alone with Sykes, Walter, and Sumersby. Glad the ordeal was over, he pushed back his chair.

"Not so fast, Trailsman," Addison said. "I'd like to have a few words with you, if you don't mind."

"About what?" Fargo asked.

The huge man placed his elbows on the table and made a tepee of his fingers. "How fond are you of Luther?"

"Fond?" Fargo asked, unsure he understood exactly what Sykes was getting at.

"Yes. How devoted are you to him? Do you feel a sense of loyalty or obligation since he's the one who hired you?"

"I have a job to do and I'll do it."

Addison tapped his forefingers against each other. "Frontier ethics, is that it? Admirable, to a degree. But it would be foolish to let your personal ethical standards prevent you from substantially increasing your net worth."

"Try that again in English," Fargo said.

"Very well. Luther told us he has agreed to pay you five thousand dollars for your services. A substantial amount for you, no doubt, but a pittance to men like us." Addison glanced at the doorway and said more quietly. "I have a proposition for you. One I think you will find to your liking."

"I'm listening."

"What would you say if Walter and I offered to pay you twice as much? Ten thousand dollars, yours to do with as you please, and no one need ever know you received it. It will be our little secret. How does that sound?"

Fargo saw Reginald Sumersby's smirk widen. "Who do you want me to shoot?"

Sykes, Walter, and Sumersby laughed, and the lawyer winked at Addison. "I told you he would go for it. Only a moron would refuse."

Addison smiled smugly. "That's just it, Mr. Fargo. You don't need to kill anyone. In fact, you don't need to do a blessed thing. Merely agree to pack up and ride out, and the ten thousand is yours."

"What about the Phantoms?" Fargo brought up. "Luther is counting on me to track them down."

"Life is full of disappointments. Luther will be upset, but in the long run it's for the best. Leave the Phantoms to us. We know how to deal with them."

To Fargo the notion was almost comical. "You've had a lot of experience with Indians, I take it?" he asked, to gauge their reaction.

Reginald Sumersby scowled, Walter averted his eyes, and Addison Sykes's tepee turned into a pair of fists. "Our expertise is not the issue here. All that should interest you is the ten thousand. What do you say? Do we have a deal? Let's shake on it and we'll turn the money over to you later. You can sneak out late tonight. No one will ever be the wiser."

"Except me," Fargo said. "And I'm the one who has to look at myself in the mirror."

Addison recoiled as if he had been punched. "You can't possibly be saying what I think you're saying."

"That I'm turning you down?" Fargo nodded. "I've already given Luther my word that I'll help him. Until he tells me different, that's exactly what I aim to do."

"You're insane," Reginald Sumersby said flatly.

"Consider carefully," Addison urged. "You're passing up more money than most men acquire in their entire lifetime. And why? Out of a juvenile sense of obligation, a misplaced moral code no intelligent person would live by."

No one had ever called Fargo moral before. He liked to drink, to gamble, to while away his nights with fallen doves. Some people would brand that as wrong, even sinful. They would say he had no morals whatsoever. But they would be wrong. There were limits to what he would do. He didn't hire out his gun for money. He didn't cheat, or lie, or steal. And he never betrayed another's trust. "I do," he said.

Reginald Sumersby snickered "I've heard of yaks like you, mister. But I never thought I would live to meet any son of a bitch stupid enough—" He stopped in utter dread.

Fargo had drawn and cocked his Colt in the blink of an eye. "You're not in Ohio anymore. Out here, if you insult a man, you better be able to back it up. I could put a slug into you and no one would blame me." He had no real intention of shooting the lawyer, but no man could abide such arrogance.

Sumersby was as pale as a bed sheet.

Rising, Fargo twirled the Colt into his holster with a flourish. "Gentlemen, it's been interesting. I look forward to our trip up into the mountains."

Addison Sykes was a study in vexation. "You only think you do. I guarantee you'll live to regret your rash decision."

"Is that a threat?"

The big man glanced at Fargo's holster. "Not at all. Consider it more in the nature of friendly advice. Your loyalty has denied you a golden opportunity. No one's word is worth ten thousand dollars. Not yours, not mine. Hell, even the President of the United States can be bought if the price is right."

Fargo hooked his thumbs in his gunbelt. "Know that for a fact?"

"Yes, Mr. Fargo, I do. Codes of honor are obsolete. They died with the age of chivalry. Money is all that matters. The real power is on Wall Street. The real rulers are those like myself who control the ebb and flow of vast wealth. You think Luther Brunsdale is rich? Compared to me, he's a pauper."

"Yet it's still not enough."

"There is no such thing as 'enough' money. The more you acquire, the more you want to acquire. And when you do, when you strike a deal worth millions, the thrill is beyond compare. It's better than the finest liquor, better than the best food, better, even, than sex."

Fargo looked at the three of them. "And you called *me* insane?" Pivoting on a boot heel, he departed. From the front of the mansion, to the right, wafted the voices of Luther and Lucy and the townsmen. Fargo turned left, down the hall to a door to the outside to get some fresh air and be alone. But he wasn't.

Light spilling from a window bathed Cleve Sneldon and Mabel, the private secretary with his hands on the maid's shoulders. He was shaking her, and she was trying to break free.

"What the hell is this?" Fargo demanded.

Sneldon snapped his arms down. "It's none of your concern! Go on about your own business."

Mabel backed toward Fargo, "One of the other maids told me she saw Mr. Sneldon go out the servants' entrance about the same time we saw that bright flash today." She smoothed her uniform. "All I did was ask him if he saw anyone out in the yard. The next thing I knew, he grabbed me and warned me to keep quiet about it, or else."

Fargo touched her shoulder. "Go inside. I'll talk to him."

The brunette nodded and left. Sneldon started to go after her, but Fargo stepped in front of him, barring his way. "Didn't you hear me? We need to talk."

"About what?" Sneldon rasped.

"This," Fargo said, and slugged him, a solid right to the stomach that folded the secretary at the waist. "That's for having those three loggers jump me this afternoon."

Gasping for breath, Sneldon whined, "It wasn't me! It was—" He bit his lower lip to keep from finishing his statement.

"It was Rem Dinsmore," Fargo said. "I know." Slipping a

hand inside Sneldon's coat, he patted the inner pocket and found a hard object, which he pulled out. "I thought so." It was a mirror five inches long and three inches wide. "I'll look up Dinsmore when we get to the line camp. In the meantime, stay away from Mabel." He tossed the mirror to the ground.

Cleve Sneldon adjusted his spectacles. "You think you're so smart, so tough. But you have no idea what you're up against. " Abruptly rotating, he ran off into the darkness.

Fargo had no inclination to give chase. As he reached for the door, mocking laughter taunted him.

"You don't know it yet, mister, but you're a dead man! You'll never come down out of those mountains alive!"

8

Shortly after nine o'clock the next morning a column of riders filed up into the Cascades from the Brunsdale estate. Luther Brunsdale wanted to leave at first light but his three guests would not cooperate. A maid had to pound on their doors repeatedly before they roused themselves from bed. They dallied over breakfast, taking an hour to eat when it should have taken them half as long. They took forever to get dressed. Finally they strolled out into the bright morning sun smiling and joking as if they were going on a picnic at an Ohio park instead of up into some of the most rugged wilderness on the continent.

Skye Fargo had a lot of time to think, and the more he thought about it, the more certain he became that Addison Sykes was up to something. Men like Sykes loved their creature comforts. For him to traipse off into the deep woods he had to have an extraordinary reason, and the one he gave just didn't ring true.

As Fargo recollected, Sykes claimed he was going to the line camp to see exactly what Luther Brunsdale was up against. Sykes had said he wanted to be fair to Luther. But it was a bold-faced lie.

Addison and Walter had been at odds with Luther for quite some time over Syke's scheme to clear-cut the forest. Luther's refusal was the real reason they wanted to oust him. They were using the attacks by the Phantoms as an excuse to vote him out. They had no real intention of playing fair with him.

They had already made up their minds.

In which case, Fargo mused, the trek to the line camp served no purpose. Addison Sykes, however, was the kind of man who had a purpose for everything he did. So the trip had to be for some other reason.

Try as he might, though, Fargo couldn't guess what it might be. So he stopped trying and concentrated on their surroundings. The forest was alive with wildlife. Sparrows frolicked at play, robins chirped merrily, squirrels scampered from limb to limb.

Fargo rode well in front of the others, alert for sign. A pair of loggers were next in line. Then came Luther, Lucy, Mabel Easy, and Cleve Sneldon, who had fought shy of Fargo all morning. Two more loggers were behind them. Addison Sykes, Walter Brunsdale, and Reginald Sumersby were next, chatting up a storm, in the best of spirits. Finally, a trio of timbermen brought up the rear.

Everyone had rifles, even Sykes, Walter, and Reginald. Fargo hoped it would deter the Phantoms from ambushing them. But he didn't relax his vigilance. He perpetually scoured the vegetation and the ground ahead.

They had been on the go no more than an hour when Walter called out, "Luther! Aren't we going to stop for a rest sometime soon? I'm terribly sore from all this riding."

"We have a long way to go, Uncle," Luther responded. "We got such a late start, we won't reach the camp until tomorrow morning. We should push on, but for your sake, we'll rest awhile."

Fargo was disappointed the timber baron gave in. Luther truly cared for his uncle, misplaced affection if ever there was any. Sliding down, Fargo moved to a spot where the slope ahead was visible. As he studied it, footsteps approached.

"Are you avoiding me, handsome?"

Fargo turned. Lucy had Mabel with her, the maid staying a discreet distance back. "What makes you say that?"

"I was expecting a knock on my door last night, but you

93

never showed," Lucy complained. "And me waiting in my new silk nightgown, too."

"I turned in early," Fargo said. Which was true. He had wanted to get together with Mabel but he didn't know where her room was.

"What does a big, strapping fellow like you need with so much sleep?" Lucy asked. "Now we won't be able to be alone together until after we return from the line camp."

Fargo changed the subject. "You need to be extra careful on this trip. The Phantoms seem to be making it a point to kill you."

Lucy laughed. "If you're trying to scare me into going back, it won't work. Fourteen others have already been killed. The savages aren't just out to get me."

Mabel took a half-step. "If I may be so bold, ma'am, you should listen to Mr. Fargo. He knows more about these things than we do."

"Oh, please. You're worse than a mother hen. I'll be perfectly fine," Lucy insisted. To Fargo she said, "You should know by now I don't scare easily. And I never let anyone keep me from doing what I want to do. Right now, I want to be with my father. He needs me and I won't let him down." She walked toward Luther.

Mabel started to go, then glanced at Fargo. "I thought you should know, Cleve Sneldon came up to me this morning during breakfast."

"I warned him to leave you alone."

"He was civil enough. He apologized for his outburst last night." Mabel checked to ensure no one was nearby. "Then he said a strange thing. He said I should learn to regard him with more respect. He said that one day soon he was going to come into a lot of money and it would be to my benefit to treat him nicely."

The secretary, Fargo saw, was talking to the lawyer, Reginald Sumersby. They made quite a pair. Two scarecrows, a pale one with spectacles, and an oily one with shifty eyes. "Did he say where the money was coming from?"

"No. I asked, and all he said was that he knew which side of the bread the butter was on. If that makes any sense." Mabel smiled sweetly. "I'd better stay close to Lucy or she might wonder what we're up to." The maid scooted off.

Fargo did a lot of wondering of his own once they were back in the saddle and climbing steadily higher. What could Sneldon have in meant? He felt as if a crucial piece of the puzzle was missing, and without it he had no hope of getting to the bottom of whatever was going on.

At noon, at Walter's insistence, they stopped again, on a broad shelf. Fargo roosted on a boulder and chewed a piece of pemmican while Luther and his partners discussed the weather and the scenery and everything except business. Lucy and Mabel were in the shade of a pine, Mabel brushing kinks out of Lucy's golden hair.

Fargo swallowed the pemmican and leaned down to pluck a stem of grass and stick it in his mouth. Suddenly he realized one of their party was missing. Cleve Sneldon was nowhere around. Rising, he moved to a small stand of firs to the south, the last spot he had seen the secretary.

Movement in the undergrowth showed where Sneldon had gone. Fargo looked back, waited until no one was paying attention to him, then darted into the trees and wound through them to a grassy area beyond.

Out in the open, gazing on up into the mountains, was Cleve Sneldon. He had pulled a pocket watch from a vest pocket and was checking the time. Replacing it, he reached inside his jacket and produced the small mirror Fargo had discovered the night before. He squinted at the sun, then experimented, holding the mirror so it would reflect the sunlight. Satisfied he had the angle right, he consulted his watch again.

Plainly, the secretary was about to signal someone. Fargo started to step past the last fir to stop him, then had second thoughts. It might be wiser to let Sneldon go through with it and maybe learn what the secretary was up to. To be forewarned was to be forearmed, as the saying went, and if an ambush lay ahead, the ambushers were in for a unwelcome surprise.

Sneldon snapped the watch shut, replaced it a second time, and raised a hand over his eyes to shield them from the glare. Intently scouring one of the ridges, he smiled and said aloud, "There we go!"

Fargo realized it was the same barren ridge on which the flash of light had appeared the day before. He observed bright gleams sparkling in sequence.

Cleve Sneldon had a habit of talking to himself "W-h-e-r-e," he spelled out the message. "Where? What the hell does he mean by that? Oh. I get it." Sneldon moved his mirror back and forth and up down, relaying his answer.

The man on the ridge responded.

"W-i-l-l-b-e-r-e-a-d-y," Sneldon said, taking it letter by letter. "Will be ready. Good for him. I can't wait to get this over with so I can take my money and leave. New York City, here I come!" The secretary chortled. "I'll live like a prince. Have a nice house, a—"

The man on the high ridge wasn't done.

"H-o-w-m-a-n-y," Sneldon said. "How many?" He worked his mirror, supplying his answer. "E-l-e-v-e-n." When no light flashed in response, he signaled again and said as he did, "A-n-y-t-h-i-n-g-e-l-s-e?"

Two fleeting gleams of light flared.

"N-o. No." The secretary shoved the mirror into his pocket. "Then it's all set. By tomorrow it will all be over."

Fargo quietly retreated into the firs, wheeled, and was back with the others well before Cleve Sneldon emerged. He headed straight for Luther but veered to the Ovaro when he saw Reginald Sumersby watching. Pretending to tighten the cinch, he bided his time, and when Sumersby and Walter began talking, he hastened over to the timber baron. "We have a problem," he announced, but not loud enough for anyone else to hear.

"It wouldn't be a normal day if we didn't," Luther said. "What is it this time?"

Keeping his back to the trio from Ohio, Fargo said, "Listen closely but don't react. We're riding into an ambush. I don't know when, I don't know where, but before the day is done, the Phantoms will jump us."

"How did you come by this information?"

"I can't say just yet." Fargo knew Brunsdale trusted Sneldon. Luther might be unwilling to accept the secretary was capable of rank treachery. "Pass the word along to your men but don't tell Sykes, your uncle, or the lawyer,"

"I can't do that. If I don't inform them, and they're killed, it would be the same as if I murdered them with my own hands."

Fargo sighed. The three buzzards were trying to force Luther out of the Syndicate, yet he put their welfare before his own. No wonder the man was so highly respected. "Do you trust me?" he asked.

"Of course."

"Then just this once do as I ask without arguing." To further convince him, Fargo said, "If it will help soothe your conscience, tell your men to do what they can to protect your uncle and the others when the Phantoms strike." Were it up to Fargo, he would just as soon let them fend for themselves.

"I don't know," Luther said. "I'm placing them in great peril. But if you insist it's the right thing to do, I'll go along with you. I only pray you know what you're doing."

Fargo thought of another precaution. "One more thing. Instruct your men to have rounds in the chambers of their rifles, and to keep their rifles handy at all times. Have them keep an eye on me. I'll let them know when the ambush is about to be sprung."

"You're taking a lot of responsibility on your shoulders."

"It's what you hired me for, isn't it?"

"Anything else?" Luther asked, and stifled a yawn. He was haggard from lack of sleep and worry.

"From here on out let me decide when we stop."

When Luther nodded, Fargo walked to the stallion and

stepped into the stirrups. "Mount up, everyone!" he directed. "We've rested long enough."

Walter Brunsdale had reclined in the grass, his chin propped on his hand, and he made no move to comply. "What impertinence. Who put you in charge?"

"Luther did," Fargo said. "So either get on your horse and come with us or head back to the house. Your choice. I don't have all day."

"You overstep yourself, sir!" Walter bristled. "I'm one of the heads of the Syndicate. If I want to rest awhile longer, that's exactly what we'll damn well do."

Addison Sykes smiled. "I wouldn't cross Walter, were I you, Fargo. He might be old, but he doesn't back down to anyone."

Reginald Sumersby had to add his two bits' worth. "Besides, what harm can another fifteen minutes do?"

Only then did it dawn on Fargo the three of them were deliberately stalling, that they had conspired all morning to delay the party as much as possible. Why they would do it was beyond him. "I'd like to reach the line camp before winter sets in," he said. "Stay here if you want, but the rest of us aren't waiting."

Luther had climbed on the bay, Lucy was astride Caesar, and Mabel was mounting her mare.

"What are you doing?" Walter addressed his nephew. "Are you going to let this frontiersman talk to me in this manner?"

"I guess I forgot to tell you, Uncle. Fargo is in charge when we're on the trail," Luther said. "He knows the wilderness and he's fought Indians before. And weren't you the one who taught me to always make the most of the abilities of those who work for me?"

Addison Sykes slowly rose. "I can see it's pointless to argue, Walter. Evidently we're to be treated like common hirelings. To avoid discord we should humor them and do as they request."

"Request, hell," Walter said as Sykes boosted him to his feet. "It was an order."

Reginald Sumersby was still on the ground. "Cave in to their demands if you want, but I refuse. I'm staying right where I am until I'm good and ready to move on. The Phantoms don't scare me. Their attacks have all taken place a lot higher up in the mountains."

Fargo was amazed by the lawyer's confidence, and puzzled as to how Sumersby knew where the Phantoms had struck before. "Do as you want. It should be safe enough. Grizzlies, mountain lions, and wolves don't usually come out at this time of day."

"Grizzlies?" Sumersby said, staring deep into the woods. "They eat people, don't they?"

"Only when they catch them." Fargo smiled. "If one tries to sneak up on you and your horse doesn't spook, you'll be all right. Usually a horse can outrun a bear."

"Usually?" Sumersby stood, trying to be casual but fooling no one. "I think I'll tag along after all."

"Suit yourself," Fargo said, reining the pinto eastward. He rode on ahead fifty yards, and paused. The others were filing up the slope after him, the trio from Ohio looking none too pleased. Grasping the Henry's stock, he hauled it from the scabbard and levered a round into the chamber, then clucked to the pinto.

Minutes became hours, the sun baking them every foot of the way. By early afternoon Fargo was caked with perspiration. It was trickling down into his eyes, stinging them. Removing his hat, he tied his bandanna around his forehead to absorb the sweat, then put his hat back on.

Most of the others were slumped in the saddle, sluggish from the heat and fatigue. Walter Brunsdale, though, was holding up well despite his age, far better than Sumersby the lawyer, who had wrapped both hands around his saddle horn as if he were afraid he would fall off

Now and then Fargo saw Lucy or Mabel gazing at him with that certain look women had, and he would smile to

himself. For all their talk about decency and modesty and la-
dylike ways, women could be more forward than men when
they hankered after a man. The trip promised to be enter-
taining in more ways than one.

By late afternoon the horses were plodding along with
their heads hung low. So were several of the loggers, Fargo
observed. If the Phantoms were to strike, his party would be
cut down before they got off a shot. Reluctantly, at the next
ridge they came to, Fargo raised an arm and called out, "We'll
give the horses a breather!"

"Thank God!" Reginald Sumersby declared. "My backside
feels as if it's been scraped raw, and my legs are cramped
stiff."

"You know who to blame," Walter Brunsdale said bitterly.

Luther did not let the comment go unchallenged. "Fargo
is only doing what he thinks is best for all of us. Be thank-
ful we've made it this far without incident."

Addison Sykes grinned. "I don't know about the rest of
you, but I'm enjoying myself immensely. I haven't spent this
much time outdoors since I was a boy. I look forward to what
lies in store for us."

Reining up beside a laurel, Fargo dismounted and tied the
reins. Trees blocked his view of the next slope so he hiked
into them in search of an opening in the canopy. Pushing his
hat back, he sought sign of the Phantoms, only to be interrupted by a rustling sound. He whirled, leveling the Henry,
and scared Mabel Easy half out of her wits.

"It's only me!"

The maid was alone. "Where's Lucy?" Fargo asked, placing the rifle's stock on the ground.

"With her father. I told her I needed a few minutes to myself." Mabel coyly clasped her hands behind her back and si-
dled nearer. "But what I really wanted was a few minutes
alone with you."

"Did you now?" Fargo asked.

Mabel stopped so close to him, her breasts nearly rubbed
his buckskin shirt. "Lucy wasn't the only one hoping you

would pay her a visit last night. I thought about slipping a note under your door inviting you to my room, but I was afraid if I were caught, it would cost me my job. So I tossed and turned in bed all night, wishing you were lying there next to me."

Fargo touched his lips. "My kisses must be more potent than I thought."

Mabel threw back her head and started to laugh, then clamped a hand over her mouth. Her body quaked with mirth, her bosom jiggling delectably, as she put a palm on his chest. "You're a terrible tease. But you're right. I couldn't stop thinking of our kiss by the hedge. I wanted a second helping."

"There's no time like the present," Fargo said, embracing her. She melted against him, her arms encircling his lower back, her tongue meeting his in a silken dance. A tiny voice in the back of Fargo's mind screamed he was being a complete idiot, that he should be on the watch for Phantoms, but he figured one little kiss couldn't hurt.

Stepping back, Mabel fanned her flushed face and giggled. "What is it about you? I'm barely able to control myself. If we were alone, I would rip your clothes off and throw you down to have my way with you."

"Promises, promises." Gazing past her, Fargo saw someone hurrying toward them, a mane of golden hair shimmering like molten ore. Raising his voice, he declared, "Yes, I've been to Denver plenty of times. They're calling it the Gateway to the Rockies."

"Denver?" Mabel said, and caught on quickly. "Yes, I've always wanted to visit there. I've heard such nice things about it."

Lucy Brunsdale wore a suspicious expression as she emerged from the pines. "Here you are, Mabel. I thought I heard you talking to someone."

"Mr. Fargo was telling me what a wonderful place Denver is," the brunette glibly fibbed. "I have an aunt who lives there and I've always wanted to visit her."

"Oh. " Lucy glanced from Fargo to the maid and back again, and visibly relaxed. "I've never been to Colorado, myself. The city I most want to visit is Rome. All those magnificent buildings, all that history. It would be a dream come true."

Fargo cradled the Henry. They shouldn't be standing around idly chatting when the Phantoms might be spying on them at that very moment. "Why don't the two of you go on back? I'll join you shortly."

"Trying to get rid of us?" Lucy asked.

"Trying to keep all of us alive," Fargo countered, and moved deeper into the woods. From the vantage of a knoll he surveyed the terrain ahead and settled on the best route to take to avoid being ambushed. Only four hours of daylight remained. The killers had to strike soon unless they were planning a surprise nighttime attack. Hoping they wouldn't, he hiked back to the rest.

Addison Sykes and Walter Brunsdale were on a log, sharing water from a water skin. Pausing with the skin halfway to his mouth, Addison said, "Look, Walter. It's the famous scout."

"And his hair is still attached to his scalp," Walter said. "Will wonders never cease."

The pair thought they were marvelously witty. Fargo was tempted to kick them both in the mouth but he contented himself with saying, "What kind of man turns on his own nephew the way you've turned on Luther?"

Walter's wrinkled face contorted as if he were sucking on a lemon. "Your presumption knows no bounds! For your information, I gave Luther every chance to come around. I pleaded again and again for him to agree to Addison's proposal. But he steadfastly refused,"

"He's telling the truth," Addison came to the older man's defense. "I would have given Luther the boot long ago were it not for Walter. He asked me to go easy. He said Luther would eventually come around."

"My mistake," Walter said. "I let blood ties blind me to

the truth. My nephew isn't half the businessman I am. He allows emotion to rule his decisions. Our visit was his last chance and he's blown it."

Disgusted, Fargo went to Luther, who was conferring with two of the loggers who had been bringing up the rear. They were unaware he was there, and he overheard one say, "— might have been someone and it might not have been. I didn't want to bother you."

"You should have informed us sooner, George," Luther said.

"About what?" Fargo made his presence known.

George was a stocky man in a flannel shirt and overalls. "About the person I might have seen an hour or so ago. I was looking back down the mountain and I thought I spotted a man watching us from an alder grove."

"And you didn't tell me?" Fargo asked, nettled by the oversight. He reminded himself the men were loggers, not soldiers.

"I wasn't sure I really saw someone," George said. "One second he was there, the next I blinked and he was gone." He shrugged. "I blamed it on a trick of the light."

Could it be? Fargo reflected. Were the Phantoms behind them instead of in front of them? Was that why he had not found any sign? The answer had to be no. Cleve Sneldon had signaled to someone up ahead, not someone lower down the mountain. "From here on out, if you see anything, anything at all, you're to let me know right away. Spread the word to the others."

"Yes, sir," George said, and he and his partner hustled off.

"If those red devils are behind us, there's no turning back even if we wanted to," Luther said. He gazed toward Lucy. "I must have been crazy to bring my daughter along. What was I thinking?"

"She would have come whether you let her or not," Fargo remarked.

"True. Knowing her, she'd have waited until were gone,

then snuck up after us and might have wound up in the clutches of the Phantoms."

"Let's head out!" Fargo proposed. Mounting the stallion, he waited for the rest to follow suit. As usual, Addison, Walter, and Sumersby took their sweet time. But at last they were ready, and he spurred into the spruce and on up the slope.

Suddenly Fargo realized the forest had gone unaccountably silent. Drawing rein, he rose in the stirrups but saw nothing out of the ordinary.

Two loggers came out of the trees to his rear. Fargo decided to stay close to the main party until they pitched camp for the night. The woods were too thick, the likelihood of an ambush too great. He turned the Ovaro sideways, looking for Lucy, Mabel, and Luther.

A second later the mountain echoed to a scream.

9

The screamer was a man, not a woman, the scream one of agonizing pain and unbridled terror.

Skye Fargo spurred the Ovaro down the slope and into the trees, passing the two loggers who had reined up and were gazing back down the mountain in mixed astonishment and fear. He was tremendously relieved to see Lucy, Mabel, and Luther ahead, unhurt, the three of them gazing toward the rear of the line.

Addison Sykes, Walter Brunsdale, Reginald Sumersby, and Cleve Sneldon were in a tight group, the latter gripping his throat in raw fright.

One of the three timbermen who had been bringing up the rear was on the ground, thrashing about with a feathered shaft protruding from his chest. The other two were on their horses, their rifles jammed to their shoulders swiveling back and forth in search of a target.

Reining up in a spray of pine needles, Fargo vaulted off and crouched beside the victim. It was George. He had stopped thrashing and was gawking skyward, his eyes as wide as his mouth. "Can you hear me?" Fargo asked.

The logger didn't say a thing. He exhaled loudly, his eyes glazing, and within seconds had expired, blood trickling from both corners of his mouth.

"Is he dead?" one of the mounted loggers inquired.

Instead of answering, Fargo snatched up George's rifle and

shoved it at the man who had asked. "Hold on to this," he ordered, and swiftly remounted.

"We didn't see a damn thing!" the other timberman declared. "We were riding along when that arrow came out of nowhere and struck poor George."

Fargo scanned the vegetation. "We'll all end up like him if we're not careful. Keep moving. If you see so much as a leaf twitch, shoot."

"But what about George? We can't just leave him here for the coyotes and buzzards to eat."

"If you want to climb down and bury him, go ahead," Fargo said. "Put down your rifle, find a stick, and start digging. Just don't turn your back to the trees."

The logger peered into the woods, bit his lip, and muttered, "Damn, damn, damn!" He rode on.

"You, too," Fargo instructed the second man. He gave the arrow stuck in George a quick scrutiny, and spurred the stallion. It was exactly like the one he had removed from Caesar's pommel, made of ash and eagle feathers with no markings to distinguish it.

The two loggers at the front of the column had recovered from their shock and trotted back to rejoin the rest. Everyone was bunched together, their rifles pointing every which way, Lucy and Mabel as grim as the rest.

"They tell me George is dead," Luther Brunsdale said as Fargo came to a stop. "How many Phantoms do you think there are?"

"There's no telling," Fargo said, turning the stallion so he faced the undergrowth. "But now we know some are behind us, and there might be more in front." He glanced at the timber baron. "You have an important decision to make."

"I know. Do we go back to the house or push on to the line camp?" Luther stared off toward the base of the Cascades, then twisted to stare up the mountain. "We're closer to the camp than to my house. If we push hard and don't stop for the night, we can get there by midnight. So I say we go on."

"Don't be ridiculous, nephew," Walter said. "What makes you think we'll be any safer there? I think we should head back down."

Luther hesitated, but Fargo didn't. "And be picked off one by one? No, Luther made the right choice. We're going on."

"You don't have any say in the matter, frontiersman," Walter sniped.

"Precisely," Addison Sykes chimed in. "As you keep conveniently forgetting, we're the bosses of this operation. We're going back whether you like it or not, and anyone who wants to join us is welcome."

To sit there arguing, with killers lurking in ambush, was folly, and Fargo said as much. "We're pushing on," he reiterated. If they split into two groups, they would be that much easier to kill.

Addison lifted his reins. "You can't stop us from doing what we want. Consider yourself fired."

Fargo swung the Henry toward him. "Consider yourself dead if you try to leave." He was bluffing but they didn't know that.

Walter Brunsdale must have been a firebrand in his youth because even in his old age he was swift to anger, and became beet red. "Do you hear him, Luther? Do you see what he is doing? Show some gumption and stand up to him before the lunatic gets us all slain."

"Fargo knows what is best, Uncle," Luther responded. "There's strength in greater numbers."

"You spineless—!" Walter fumed, but got no further.

Out of one eye Fargo glimpsed motion among the spruce. Shifting, he banged off two swift shots at the selfsame moment an arrow streaked out of the greenery. He couldn't say if he hit the bowman or not.

The arrow flashed toward one of the loggers. But as luck would have it, the man's horse was frightened by the Henry's blast and pranced sideways. In so doing, it saved the logger's life, causing the shaft to miss him.

The arrow thudded into Reginald Sumersby's chest instead.

Stunned disbelief riveted the others as the lawyer looked down at the arrow jutting from his body. "It's not supposed to happen like this," he said. Then his body melted from under him and he pitched headfirst from the saddle.

"No!" Addison Sykes cried, scrambling off his own animal. "This can't be! It just can't be!"

Fargo stayed on the Ovaro, covering the brush, There was nothing he could do for the lawyer, and anyone who turned their back to the Phantom might well be the next to die.

Addison sank onto his knees and propped the lawyer's head on his legs. "Sumersby? Sumersby? Don't die on us!"

But Reginald Sumersby already had. His eyes were blank slates, his chest wasn't moving, and a bright scarlet rivulet dribbled down over his thin lower lip and across his pointed chin.

"This is horrible, just horrible!" Walter said. "How could it all go so wrong?" He shook himself, as if rousing from a stupor, and said, "Addison, it's all gone to hell. We need to go on, just as they want. It's not safe to try and go back."

Sykes's jowls were quivering. Elevating both knobby fists over his head, he let out with the roar of an enraged beast. "There will be a reckoning!" he thundered at the sky. "I swear to heaven there will!"

Lucy had been uncommonly quiet, but now she said, "Save your silly theatrics for later. The longer we sit here like bumps on a damn log, the greater the chance more of us will wind up like your friend,"

Glaring balefully, Addison rose and climbed on his horse.

Cleve Sneldon, Fargo saw, was gaping at Sumersby in horror. When one of the other horses bumped against his own, he jumped as if startled, then gulped and looked around him in blatant dread.

Fargo moved past him. "Did something go wrong?" he could not resist asking. Pushing to the front, he barked instructions. "Ride in twos! Each of you keep an eye on one side of the trail, and watch each other's backs. Stay close but don't bunch up."

They hurriedly paired off, the remaining loggers choosing one another. Naturally, Addison and Walter did the same. Sneldon and a logger were behind them. Lucy moved next to her father.

That left Mabel without a partner. Slapping her legs against the mare, she rode up next to Fargo. "I guess it's you and I."

"Do you know how to use that thing?" Fargo nodded at her rifle.

"I hunted grouse and quail with my father when I was younger," the maid said. "I may not be the best shot in the world, but if anyone tries to kill me, I'll be damned if I'm not gonna get off a shot or two first."

Their plight notwithstanding, Fargo smiled. "You'll do to ride the river with."

"What's that mean?"

"Tell you later," Fargo said. It was an expression cowboys in general, and Texans in particular, were fond of, and it was the highest compliment they could pay another person. "We have to head out." He glanced at the others to verify they were ready, and tapped his spurs against the pinto.

In somber silence they climbed rapidly, the woods around them as still as a cemetery. The heavy thud of their animals' hooves resounded dully like the heavy tread of boots in a tomb. Slabs of trees towered overhead, row after uneven row of wide trunks and slender boles. Thick clumps of weeds and clusters of high grass offered enough hiding places for a horde of archers.

Each second seemed like a minute, each minute like an hour. They never knew when another shaft would whisk out of nowhere to transfix another victim. Jumpy, on edge, they snapped their rifles at shadows.

Fargo was perplexed when the Phantoms didn't try to drop a few more of them. Either the killers were playing it safe, or they had something special in mind. He suspected he knew what it was. Barely three hours of daylight were left. Once darkness descended, it would be child's play for the bushwhackers to sneak in close and pick the party off at their leisure.

"Do you reckon we'll make it?" Mabel abruptly wanted to know.

"Either we will, or we'll die trying," Fargo said.

The maid cracked a grin. "There's optimism for you. But what you're really saying is that it will be a miracle if any of us get out of this alive." She regarded the wall of plant life before them. "I've always loved these mountains. I never expected to die in them."

"Now who's being optimistic?"

Another half an hour dragged by. Another thirty minutes of tense, anxious, nerve-fraying travel,

Fargo's neck became stiff from constantly crooking it from side to side and front to back. They needed to stop, to rest, to stretch, but they dared not. It might be just what the Phantoms were waiting for.

"Cleve Sneldon sure looks scared," Mabel commented. "He's as white as whitewash and keeps wringing his hands."

"It's not going the way he thought it would," Fargo remarked, That, and the man had a yellow streak down his spine as wide as the Mississippi River.

"How's that?" Mabel asked.

"Tell you later," Fargo said again.

The brunette chuckled. "You sure have an awful lot to explain. But I want to do a lot more than just talk to you."

"Show me."

"Here and now? In front of everyone?" Mabel said, and giggled. "You're teasing me. Don't you worry, though. I'll show you when the time comes."

The forest thinned. A steep slope, littered with boulders lay before them. Above it was a notch through a heavily timbered bench.

"Can I ask you a question?"

"I never refuse a lady," Fargo responded. They were relatively safe for the moment. But he didn't like the looks of that notch. Not one bit.

"Do you ever think about dying? About what it will be like? I never did, not until the Phantoms went on their blood-thirsty spree. I always figured I would live to a ripe old age, and either die in my sleep or in a rocking chair, knitting. But that's not how it works, is it? We can die at any time, anywhere, without any warning whatsoever."

"Afraid so," Fargo said. It was a lesson some never learned. Incredibly enough, there were people who went through life thinking they were invincible, that all they had to do was believe they wouldn't die, and they wouldn't. Silliness, plain and simple, and it wasn't limited to whites. Fargo had met warriors who firmly believed their medicine bags would protect them from all harm. Some even went so far as to think they were bulletproof.

"When our lives can end at any minute," Mabel was saying, "it makes each moment we live more special, more precious."

Fargo was thinking of something else. A single arrow had killed George; a single arrow had slain Sumersby. So there might only be one Phantom behind them. If so, once they were through the notch, he could slip into the trees and turn the tables by lying in ambush for the ambusher.

"Say, Fargo!" Walter Brunsdale chose that juncture to call out. "Is there any chance of us stopping for a while? I'm tired, truly tired."

There was no denying the older man appeared peaked, but Fargo responded, "Not just now. We're not out of danger yet."

"Coming to this godforsaken territory was the biggest mistake I've ever made," Walter stated to no one in particular. "Sumersby would still be alive if I hadn't insisted on giving my nephew a last chance to change his mind."

Addison flicked a speck of dust from his jacket. "How many times have I warned you about letting sentiment warp your judgment? A businessman can't permit emotion to influence his decisions."

"I apologize for my shortcoming," Walter said. "From now

on, the Syndicate is all that matters. I'll gladly go along with whatever you want to do."

"You can't realize how glad that makes me, old friend," Addison Sykes said. "My goal now is to punish those responsible for this outrage and set things right. I do not countenance failure or stupidity."

Some of the loggers were listening to the partners instead of concentrating on what they should be doing. "Stay alert!" Fargo shouted to remind them. Hardly were the words out of his mouth than an arrow shot like a bolt out of the blue into the back of one of the timbermen and the man cried out and toppled, his arms flung out from his sides.

It was more than the others could take. Almost to a man, they turned and opened fire, pouring a stream of hot lead into the woods, shooting wildly, recklessly. The slugs sheared leaves and sent slivers of wood flying.

"Stop!" Fargo yelled. "You're wasting your ammunition." But he was drowned out by the din, by blast after blast as they fired and fired and fired until their rifles went empty and their hammers clicked dry.

The Phantom had been waiting for just that moment. Another shaft sped true, thunking into the back of the timberman next to Cleve Sneldon. Screeching in dismay, the secretary fled up the slope in blind panic, madly lashing his horse with the reins. His hysteria was contagious.

Bellowing "Run for your lives!," one of the remaining loggers broke into a gallop. Addison and Walter immediately joined the flight. Not to be left behind, Luther and Lucy sped after them, and the rest streamed along.

Fargo and Mabel were the only two who held their ground. Then it was just Fargo. Lucy bawled at the maid to flee, and Mabel, without thinking, took flight. "No! Don't!" Fargo hollered, but they didn't hear him and wouldn't stop if they had. All he could do was try to overtake them.

Cleve Sneldon was barreling toward the shaded notch at a breakneck pace, the others following his lead.

Rocks clattered from under the Ovaro's hooves. The steep

slope hindered the stallion, slowing it down, and although Fargo caught up with Mabel, he couldn't possibly catch the rest before they reached the top. No one was pursuing them, which didn't surprise him. The wily killer was too smart to show himself.

Sneldon was almost to the top and showed no inclination to slow down. He had lost his hat but he didn't care. His legs flapping, he rounded a boulder, came to a patch of loose pebbles, and nearly went down when his mount floundered.

Some of the others were having trouble, too, but they didn't let that stop them. They had lost all reason, all common sense.

The secretary hurtled pell-mell into the notch, out of Fargo's sight. A logger was next, with Addison, Walter, Luther, and Lucy close behind.

Fargo was the only one who kept an eye on the timber flanking it. He was the only one who spied movement, the only one who realized they had done exactly as the Phantoms wanted and had blundered into an ambush. "Look out!" he roared, but no one listened.

Gunfire boomed. Rifles and pistols spewed a deluge of lead and smoke. Fargo heard horses squeal, heard screams and cries and curses. Clenching his teeth in fury, he flew toward the opening and burst up over the rim not knowing what he would find.

Two horses were down, one kicking and convulsing in a spreading pool of blood. A logger was nearby, his body bent at an unnatural angle. Another logger had been unhorsed but was on his feet, bleeding profusely from several wounds as he flung slugs at the men hidden above them.

Of Cleve Sneldon there was no trace. Walter Brunsdale's horse was rearing and plunging and he was desperately struggling to regain control. Addison had stopped to help him but there was little he could do. Luther was slumped over his saddle, his features twisted in torment, while Lucy and Mabel and the last two timbermen were pouring fire at the Phantoms.

A slap of Fargo's legs brought the Ovaro into the thick of the frenzy. He spotted a vague shape in the brush, fixed a hasty bead, and smoothly stroked the trigger. "We have to get out of here!" he shouted to be heard above the clamor.

"My father has been hit!" Lucy cried.

"Take him and go!" Fargo said, snapping a shot at another shadowy form. A slug buzzed close to his cheek, another nicked his left sleeve but didn't crease his flesh. He fired at both slopes, working the Henry nonstop, and for several moments the hail of bullets tapered, long enough for Lucy to grab the reins to her father's bay and take flight eastward with Mabel right behind her.

Addison Sykes had succeeded in seizing the reins to Walter's mount and imitated their example.

Only Fargo and two loggers were left. The man with the multiple wounds had fallen and was twitching in his death throes. "Ride! Ride!" Fargo commanded, but before either logger could obey, the face of the timberman on Fargo's left dissolved in a spray of gore.

Up in the trees a Phantom stepped into view, taking steady aim with his rifle. Fargo shot first, his slug slamming into the bushwhacker's head and jolting him backward. For an instant Fargo saw the man clearly, and the fury he had felt before was nothing compared to the cold fury that gripped him now.

The last logger was galloping for cover. Fargo fired a final shot and dogged the man's hooves. They were almost to the forest when several rifles cracked simultaneously and the logger arched his spine and keeled to the right. Lead sought Fargo, too, missing by a whisker, and then he was in among the firs and riding hell-bent after the others.

Lucy and Mabel had halted less than forty yards away. Fargo saw Addison Sykes and Walter speed by them without so much as a glance. Slowing, he shoved the Henry into the saddle scabbard and palmed his Colt. "We can't stop yet!" he said as he came abreast of the women. "They'll be after us."

"I need to see how bad off my father is," Lucy said, about to climb down.

Luther Brunsdale lifted his head. He was in acute anguish, with a red stain marking his jacket and shirt. "Listen to Fargo. I'll be all right. It's just my shoulder."

"I want to see for myself," Lucy insisted.

Fargo glanced back. Men were bounding from the timber toward them. "We don't have time for this!" he declared, and slapped the bay on the flank. The animal took off as if shot from a cannon.

"Damn you!" Lucy said, chasing after it.

To discourage the Phantoms, Fargo twisted and fired twice. Mabel had bravely waited for him, and as he applied his spurs, she brought the mare alongside the stallion.

Conversation was impossible. The woods were too dense, too choked with obstacles. For over a mile their flight continued, until they came to a clearing and discovered Luther Brunsdale on his back on the ground and Lucy on her knees next to him, prying at his bloodstained shirt.

Fargo hauled on the reins and was out of the saddle before the pinto fully stopped. Sinking down on Luther's other side, he said, "We can only spare a few minutes."

"I'll take as long as is necessary," Lucy responded. When she exposed the wound, she winced as if she were the one who had been shot.

Fargo bent lower. The slug had entered just below Luther's collarbone and exited out his back. The exit hole was the size of an apple but the bone was not broken and the wound had almost stopped bleeding. He would need weeks to mend, and he would be sore for months after that, but he would live.

Lucy looked at the maid, "We must bandage him. Break out the medical kit from your saddlebag, Mabel."

"Not yet," Fargo said. "Let's go another mile." At least. Unless he missed his guess, the Phantoms were not going to give up until all of them were worm food.

Neither woman acknowledged he existed. Mabel hopped down with the kit in hand and knelt beside Lucy. As efficiently as a skilled nurse, she commenced to clean the wound, front and back, and spread healing ointment.

Rising, Fargo yanked the Henry out and began to reload. "Hurry it up," he urged. "I won't be able to hold them all off by myself"

"Then ride on if you want," Lucy said testily. "Although I never took you for the kind of man to run out on friends."

Women and mules, Fargo mused, had a lot in common. "I won't run out on you," he assured her while scouring the woodland to the west, "but I don't care to die, either, if I can help it."

"When we hear them coming, we'll leave," Lucy said. "Not before."

Luther had been dazedly listening to their exchange. Weakly placing a hand on his daughter's arm, he said, "Do as he says. He's trying to save our lives."

"Hush up!" Lucy said. "You're delirious, Father. You don't know what you're talking about."

"I am perfectly lucid," Luther said. "You're the one being her usual stubborn self. Don't blame Fargo."

Mabel, meanwhile, had taken a long cotton bandage from the kit and was gingerly wrapping it around the timber baron's shoulder. "This will hurt a little," she apologized. "But I'll be done soon."

"I can't wait to catch up to Addison and Walter," Lucy growled. "Did you see what they did? Rode right on by us without bothering to stop. They're both as cowardly as that miserable Sneldon."

Luther turned his misery-seared face to Fargo. "How many of my men made it through the gap?"

"None," Fargo said. They were fortunate *any* of them had. If the bushwhackers had been better shots, they wouldn't have. The Phantom behind them had been the real threat, as deadly as he was with both a rifle and a bow.

"Dear God," Luther said sadly. "This senseless slaughter has to stop."

"It will, Father," Lucy replied, "Wait and—" Suddenly

stiffening, she speared a finger to the north. "Skye! Behind you!"

Spinning around, Fargo beheld five figures flitting through the forest toward them.

10

Skye Fargo jammed the Henry to his right shoulder and curled back the hammer to shoot. But when he sighted down the barrel at the foremost of the onrushing figures, he titled the barrel up and let the hammer down again instead of squeezing the trigger. "It's all right," he told Luther, Lucy, and Mabel. "They're on our side."

Out of the woods loped the Hanken clan. In the lead was old Seth, his long Kentucky rifle clutched in both gnarled hands. Strung out in his wake were Orville, Harry, Josiah, and Theodore. The elder Hanken came to a stop and declared, "Well, I'll be tarred and feathered! When we heard all the ruckus, we never figured you folks were involved."

"Am I glad to see you," Fargo said, and meant it. With their help he could not only hold off the Phantoms, he could end the reign of terror.

"Mr. Brunsdale! You've been shot!" Seth went over and hunkered. "Who did this? How bad are you?"

Lucy answered. "It was the Phantoms, He'll live, but we need to get him to the line camp as soon as possible."

Hanken's four sons had stopped short at the sight of the women and were shyly ogling them without trying to be too apparent.

Fargo surveyed the terrain to the west. As yet there was no sign of the killers but he was sure they would show. They knew they had hit Luther, and they would want to finish him off. As briefly as possible, he related the clash to Seth.

"Lordy," the old man said, standing. "You folks were powerful lucky. If you think they're still after you, we should make a stand right here. We'll give the scum a taste of their own medicine and ambush *them* for a change."

"My thinking exactly," Fargo agreed, nodding. "I want you and your sons to spread out and—"

"Hold it right there!" Lucy jumped to her feet, stepped over Luther, and marched up to them. "My father's welfare comes before all else. We're heading for camp, and the six of you will protect him every foot of the way."

"But if the Phantoms come after us, we can end it," Fargo said.

"And risk having my father shot a second time? I should say not. Saving him is all that matters. We need to get him into a warm bed and doctor him day and night."

Seth nodded at his sons. "How about if I send a couple of my boys back with you, Miss Brunsdale, while the rest of us stay to lend Fargo a hand?"

"And what if more savages jump us along the way? No. I want all of you to go along," Lucy stated with finality. "Now give us a hand boosting my father up."

Against his better judgment Fargo gave in. As much as he wanted to bring the Phantoms to bay, Lucy had a valid point. Safeguarding Luther was crucial. Were he to die, Addison Sykes and Walter could do as they pleased with the Timber Syndicate. It would spare them the necessity of publicly ousting him.

In short order they were underway. Seth had Orville and Harry bring up the rear, while he took the other two boys a dozen yards ahead.

Lucy rode next to Luther, who was slumped over but able to stay in the saddle. Whenever he swayed, however slightly, she instantly put a hand on his shoulder to steady him.

Fargo and Mabel rode side-by-side. They had not gone far when she said quietly, "You know, it's a funny thing. I got a look at one of the Phantoms during the fight. Not a good look, mind you, just a glimpse, is all, but I would be

119

willing to swear on a stack of Bibles that the man I saw wasn't an Indian. He was white." She looked at him. "Is it possible? Or was I mistaken?"

"Anything is possible." Fargo was unwilling to commit himself just yet. He still needed proof. If he told her, she might tell the Brunsdales, or Rem Dinsmore.

"All those good men, dead," Mabel said sorrowfully. "I knew some of those loggers personally. They were rough around the edges but fine gentlemen nonetheless, and they always treated me with respect." She reached up to fiddle with her bun, which had become partly undone. "I can't say I'll miss Mr. Sumersby very much, though. He was one of the rudest, most spiteful people I've ever met."

"You're being polite," Fargo said. "Sumersby was a rotten son of a bitch, and his death is the one good thing that came out of this mess."

"My, my," Lucy said, forcing a grin. "I didn't realize you had such a mean streak. Or do you only get this way when your dander is up?"

Before Fargo could respond, Lucy Brunsdale looked back at them. "When we reach the line camp, I'll have Rem send an armed party to reclaim the bodies of the men who were killed. Then I'm dispatching a rider to the settlement. I want every available man up here within three days, Not just lumbermen. I want every farmer, every townsman. I'm also sending a message to the chief of the Calapooyans to demand he send some of his warriors. By the time I'm done, I'll have a small army at my disposal. Enough to wipe out the Phantoms to the last warrior."

Fargo knew it would be wasted effort. He also knew he would be wasting his breath if he tried to talk her out of it.

Mabel brought up something else. "Has anyone given any thought to where Cleve, Mr. Sykes, and Walter got to? They're not very familiar with these mountains. Do you think they will reach camp safely?"

"I hope they don't," Lucy hissed. "After what Sneldon did, it would serve him right if he became hopelessly lost.

He won't last three days on his own. As for my father's despicable partners, they can rot in hell for all I care."

Luther Brunsdale stirred. "Now, now, daughter. I'll have none of that talk. Despise them if you must, but don't allow your hatred to make you bitter. They're merely doing what they believe is best for them and for the Syndicate. As Addison mentioned, it's not personal, it's business."

Lucy was incredulous. "How can you defend them? They're out to destroy you. Yes, I'm bitter, and I make no apologies, either."

A little color had returned to Luther's cheeks, but he was still much too pale, and slick with sweat. Licking his lips, he said, "First off, they only want to remove me, not destroy me. If they succeed, it won't be the end of the world. I can probably get a job working for Governor Whiteaker. He offered me a position in his administration, you'll recall, when he took office. He says I'm a natural for politics. There was even talk of my running for Congress. But I turned him down, The Timber Syndicate is my first love."

"Which is why we can't stand by and let Sykes and Walter steal it out from under you," Lucy said. "We should contact the governor and have him intervene on your behalf."

"I'm afraid there's nothing he can do," Luther said. "What Addison and Walter are doing is perfectly legal."

"But it's wrong, Father. We can have the governor put pressure on them. Have him tell them he prefers to have you stay on as head of the Syndicate. They'll think twice if it puts them on bad terms with the State government."

Luther smiled. "My little tigress. I appreciate your feelings, but I'm not about to impose on Governor Whiteaker. This is between Addison, Walter, and myself Whatever the outcome, I will conduct myself responsibly and maturely."

Lucy was close to tears, "Damn you and your decency! Sometimes I don't understand you at all. You're willing to let them stab you in the back, willing to let them destroy everything you've spent your life building."

"What will be, will be, daughter. Fretting over it serves no purpose."

"You're wrong, Father, I love you dearly, but you're wrong. I believe we make our own destiny. I believe we should stand up to people like Sykes and Walter. Fight fire with fire. Do to them as they're doing to us."

Fargo agreed with her. He had never been one to let others impose on him. Meekly turning the other cheek wasn't part of his nature. If it was, he would have been dead a long time ago. The world was chock full of cutthroats and hardcases who had no qualms about slitting the throat of anyone who dared stand up to them. Ruthless, greedy manipulators like Addison Sykes, who did whatever they had to in order to get their way. Men who ground others under their heel like bugs. Unless someone stood up to them, unless someone was willing to meet the Sykeses of the world on their own terms, soon there wouldn't be any meek folk left to inherit anything.

The shadows around them lengthened as the sun dipped lower and lower. Soon a blazing rosy crown was all that remained, and Seth Hanken ran back to ask, "Do we make camp, or keep going, Miss Brunsdale? It's up to you."

"We push on," Lucy said. "We're not stopping until my father is safe. I don't care if we're up half the night."

"I reckoned as much," Seth said, and moved past her to fall into place beside the Ovaro. "I thought you should know why we didn't stay at the camp and watch over things like you told me to."

"You must have had a reason," Fargo said.

"The best. The morning after you left, someone started taking potshots at the loggers. It was just one fella, near as I could tell. He'd shoot, then run off into the woods. Just when things quieted down, there would be another shot, and another logger would drop. My boys and me always went after him but he always outfoxed us and we lost his trail."

"How long did this go on?"

"Until yesterday afternoon. It got so no one could step

outside for fear of being shot dead in their tracks. Most of the timbermen are holed up in the bunkhouse and the cookhouse." Seth paused. "Seven killed and six wounded, some of them serious. The loggers have about had enough. Some are ready to call it quits but Rem Dinsmore talked them into staying on awhile yet."

"Anything else?" Fargo prompted when he saw the Tennessean had more to say but was hesitant to do so.

"The strangest thing, friend. I don't know what to make of it. I saw Dinsmore talking to three of the loggers who were shot not more than fifteen minutes before each of them was gunned down. Twice the first day, once the next." Seth scratched his stubbly chin. "I didn't think much of it until that third time. But it was awful peculiar."

That it was, Fargo reflected.

"Anyway, my boys and me have been doing what we could to protect the workers. We were out searching for sign when we heard all the shooting a while ago and came for a look-see. Good thing we did."

"You've done the best anyone could," Fargo said. "I have no complaints."

"Coming from a jasper like you, that's saying a lot." Grinning, Seth touched his hat brim to Mabel and ran to rejoin Josiah and Theodore.

"You like him, don't you?" the brunette asked.

"Why wouldn't I?"

"Most of the settlers and the loggers look down their noses at the Hankens. They call them bumpkins and poke fun at them behind their back." Mabel stared after the old man. "Yet here they are, risking their necks to help the very people who belittle them."

"Next to Lucy and her father, they're the only ones you can trust."

"Trust how? None of the timbermen have ever mistreated me. Quite the opposite. I trust them, too."

She had missed the point, but Fargo didn't elaborate. He noticed how her dress had hitched up her legs as she rode, revealing a tantalizing glimpse of creamy thigh above her knee. He found himself imagining how smooth her skin must be, how nice it would be to run his hand over it. Shaking himself, he derailed the train of thought and focused on staying alive

The sun was gone. Twilight rapidly deepened. A few stars sparkled to life and soon multiplied.

With the advent of night, predators would venture from their lairs and dens to prowl for prey. Fargo was concerned the scent of dried blood on Luther Brunsdale's clothes might lure a wandering grizzly or mountain lion. About ninety minutes after sunset he heard the guttural grunt of a bear to the north, but whether it was a silver-tip or a black bear was impossible to tell. Whatever it was, it did not come any closer, which was fine by him.

Not long after, there was a commotion up ahead, excited voices and then the clomp of hooves. Fargo rode past the Brunsdales and leveled the Henry. In a few moments Seth and his two younger sons came out of the trees guiding three figures on horseback.

"Look at what we found."

Addison Sykes, Walter Brunsdale, and Cleve Sneldon looked as if they had been through hell and back again. Sneldon, in particular, was haggard and disheveled, his jacket torn, his pants ripped.

"You three!" Lucy cried, bringing up her rifle. "I should shoot you down like curs for running out on us!"

Luther unfurled, grimacing in pain. "No!" He grabbed the barrel of her gun and pushed it aside. "That would be cold-blooded murder."

"So?" Lucy responded. "They have it coming. They deserve it."

'No one ever deserves to die," her father said.

Addison Sykes was his usual unflappable self. "I'm glad to see one of you is thinking clearly. Listen to your father, Miss Brunsdale. Kill me and you will spend the rest of your days behind bars." He brazenly brought his horse up close to hers. "And I'll have you know I didn't run out on anyone. Your uncle's mount was out of control and nearly threw him. I saved his life by getting out of there before he came to harm."

"That's right," Walter defended his partner. "If it weren't for Addison, I would be lying back there with the others."

"What's your excuse?" Lucy demanded of Cleve Sneldon.

The private secretary squirmed in the saddle. "I don't have one. I'll admit I was scared. But you can't hold it against me. I'm not like Fargo. I'm not a gunman or an Indian fighter. I've never killed anyone. Hell, I've never shot at another human being my whole life."

"So you deserted us," Lucy said, contempt oozing from every pore. "You saved your own hide, not caring one whit about what happened to ours."

"What else would you have had me do?" Sneldon countered. "Stick around waiting for the bullet with my name engraved on it?"

Luther held a hand up. "Enough of this petty bickering. Let's move on. We still have eight or nine miles to go."

"It's fortuitous you came along when you did," Addison said. "We were hopelessly lost. We were about to bed down and wait until morning to try and find the camp. Cleve was attempting to start a fire when Mr. Hanken and his sons found us." He looked down at Seth. "With that accent, I take it you're from the south. Backwoodsmen, I gather? How ironic men of our station should be rescued by men of yours."

"Yes, we're Southerners and damn proud of it," Seth said. "And we don't cotton to being called names."

"My apologies, sir," Addison said drolly.

Not one of them, Fargo observed, bothered to ask how Luther was doing. Not even Luther's uncle, the one he thought so highly of. "We're heading east. Follow Seth and his sons. We'll be right behind you." The last thing he wanted was them at his back.

No one had much to say after that. Hour after hour they

plodded higher up into the Cascades, their horses as tired as they were. Out of habit, Fargo marked the time by the position of the constellations. Midnight came and went. One A.M. Two. Finally, in the distance, pinpoints of light gleamed.

"We're almost there," Fargo said for the maid's benefit. Her chin had been drooping, her eyes closing for longer and longer spells, but the news snapped her fully awake.

"Finally!" Mabel exclaimed. "Safe at last."

Nothing could be farther from the truth. Not after Fargo had seen one of the Phantoms. He was the only one who had any inkling that riding into the line camp was the same as riding into a nest of vipers.

"Before I forget, and just so you'll know," Mabel whispered, "I have a small room all to myself at the back of the house. It's not much. A bed and a closet and a dresser. My bedroom door is the one nearest the back door."

"Is that an invitation?"

"Would you prefer it in writing?" Mabel grinned. "Feel free to pay me a visit any time of the day or night."

The others spied the lights. Cleve Sneldon whooped for joy. Addison and Walter talked about how marvelous it would be to crawl into a bed and sleep for days. Lucy rode faster, anxious for her father. And the Hankens gathered next to the Ovaro, Seth asking, "Do we go out hunting for the Phantoms come daylight?"

"No," Fargo said. It would be pointless to go searching for them when the killers were right under their very noses. "Look me up about nine." By then he might have an idea of how to go about exposing the Phantoms for who they truly were.

Sentries had been posted, as they learned when an inky silhouette materialized and a harsh voice rang out, "Who the hell is out there? Speak quick before I spray you with lead!"

"It's me and my boys, Sam," Seth hollered. "And we've got Mr. Brunsdale and a bunch of others with us. Mr. Brunsdale is bad hurt."

"I'll fetch Rem," Sam said, and raced toward the tents.

A general uproar resulted. Once the bull of the woods was roused from sleep, he bellowed for others, and before long the entire camp was astir. Loggers in various states of undress rushed to greet their employer. Rem Dinsmore helped Lucy ease her father from the bay and braced Luther as he shuffled to the door.

"Hold up a moment," Luther said, faced around, silencing the hubbub. "I'll keep this short. We lost some good men today. George Flanders, Pete Wilson, and others." Luther winced but persevered, "I've heard about the men who were shot while I was gone. And I want you to know I'll do all in my power to stop the bloodshed once and for all."

A hearty cheer went up, the loggers whooping and yipping as if they had just struck it rich.

The effort cost Luther and he sagged, but Rem Dinsmore supported him and thundered, "Go back to bed for now! We'll call a meeting just as soon as Mr. Brunsdale is up to it."

Lucy started to sidle her father through the doorway, then she stopped and glanced at Fargo and the Syndicate partners. "We have two spare bedrooms. Skye, you can have one. Mr. Sykes and Walter will have to share the other."

"Don't be preposterous," Addison said in amazement. "You can't really expect Walter and I to share the same bed."

"Or one of you can sleep on the floor. I honestly don't give a damn," Lucy said, "Your room is the second on the left, Fargo's is the last one on the right."

"Well, I never," Walter spat.

The partners were not the only ones unhappy with the arrangement. "You're letting the high-and-mighty scout sleep in the same house with you?" Rem Dinsmore said. "It's not proper."

"Don't start," Lucy warned.

"He can share a tent with the men. Or I'll have one of the boys give up their bunk in the bunkhouse for the night," Rem proposed.

"I'm in no mood for your childishness," Lucy warned.

"He's my father's guest and he'll sleep in here. Now help me get my father inside."

Mabel winked at Fargo and hurried to assist her mistress and the camp foreman, whispering as she walked off, "I'm directly across from you."

Fargo reined the stallion on around to the rear of the building. Dismounting, he stripped off the saddle and saddle blanket and deposited them next to the rear door. The saddlebags he took with him. Pressing on the latch, he entered a narrow hall, From the bedroom nearest the parlor Lucy's voice drifted.

The door to the room he had been given was halfway open, and Fargo left it that way. He tossed the saddlebags and the Henry on the bed and sat on the edge in the dark, fully intending to catch some sleep. Surprisingly, though, his fatigue had evaporated. He lay back anyway, his hands behind his head.

For a while the hallway bustled with activity. Fargo heard Lucy send Mabel to fetch a basin of hot water and fresh bandages. While the maid was gone, Lucy and Rem Dinsmore had a heated dispute over the propriety of her allowing Fargo to spend the night. Dinsmore wouldn't let the matter drop until Luther Brunsdale took a hand by declaring sternly, "That's enough out of you, Rem! Thank you for helping me inside. Now it would be wise for you to leave."

"But Mr. Brunsdale, what if you need me during the night? Maybe I should stick around until morning."

"Leave, Rem. Now," Luther commanded.

Rem asked Lucy to see him to the door but she declined. Fargo heard the tromp of the big man's heavy boots recede toward the front door, followed by the crash of the door being slammed.

"That was no way to treat your foreman," Walter Brunsdale said. "He only has your best interests at heart."

"Yet another example of how your ability to lead has eroded," Addison Sykes remarked. "The situation required tact and diplomacy, yet you booted Dinsmore out as if he were a drunken lout."

"And now I'm doing the same with both of you," Luther said. "I want to be alone with my daughter."

Fargo listened to shoes scrape in the hall, then Walter saying, "It's a shame you wouldn't accept the inevitable, nephew. There's no bucking progress, as you'll learn to your sorrow soon enough."

A door closed, and for a while the muted voices of Walter and Addison Sykes droned like the buzzing of bees. Eventually the buzzing ceased, and not long after loud snoring took its place.

Fargo tried to drift off, but his mind was racing faster than an antelope. He sat up when he heard Mabel say, "Good night, ma'am. I'll be up at five and have breakfast prepared by six." The rustle of her dress coincided with a shadow passing his doorway, and he rose and padded over.

Mabel had opened her door and was looking over her shoulder into his room. Spying him, she grinned and nodded and went in, her hips swaying suggestively. She left her door cracked several inches.

Fargo removed his spurs, placed them on the dresser, and poked his head out. A rosy glow bathed the hall its entire length thanks to a lantern on a peg at the far end. He quietly shut his door behind him, slipped into the maid's room, and just as quietly closed her door behind him, too.

Mabel had shed her brown uniform and was reclining on her bed in her underthings, her back propped against a pillow, a knee crooked seductively. She had let her hair down and it spilled past her shoulders in a fine brown wave. "I was starting to think you had changed your mind."

"You don't know me very well," Fargo quipped, For that matter, she didn't know men very well. Unless a man was on his deathbed, he would sooner have his limbs hacked off with a rusty sword than pass up the chance to be with a woman. Crossing to the bed, he took off his gunbelt.

Mabel held a palm out. "Not so fast, handsome. We need

to be careful. Keep the noise down. No moaning, no scream-
ing, no playful talk. Do you think you can handle that?"

"Do you?" Fargo rejoined, and lowered himself toward
her.

11

Skye Fargo felt a stirring below his belt as he stretched out on the small bed beside Mabel Easy's luscious body. She eagerly opened her slender arms and hungrily melted against him, her pert, strawberry-hued lips parting in anticipation. Fargo fastened his mouth on hers. Her warm breath was like a blast of hot desert air. Her agile tongue glided over and around his, enticing him with her sweet, heady taste.

Mabel was considerably shorter than Lucy, her body much more compact. Her shoulders were broader yet smoothly feminine, her breasts pert and firm with long nipples that jutted like twin nails. Her hips flared above thighs made muscular by all the hours she spent on her feet working. She had fuller cheeks and a higher forehead but her eyes smoldered with the same intense desire.

Fargo sucked on her tongue and had his sucked on in turn. One of her hands was at the nape of his neck tickling the short hairs, her other hand was exploring his hard frame, roving from his broad chest down over his stomach to his legs. She was not quite as bold as Lucy and stopped short of his rising pole.

Since they had to be quiet, Mabel didn't moan or groan. She did utter tiny gasps and mews from time to time. When Fargo parted her silky undergarment to free a swollen breast and swooped his mouth to her nipple, Mabel arched her spine and opened her mouth wide as if to scream but no sound came out.

Her entire body was hot to the touch, as if she were a fireplace ember. Fargo caressed her thighs, but did not yet touch her innermost recess. He nibbled on her nipple and tweaked it between his lips. Cupping her other mound, he kneaded it as a sculptor would knead clay, causing Mabel to bite her lower lip. Her nails dugs into the back of his neck, but they were much shorter than Lucy's and didn't hurt half as much.

Fargo lathered her breast with his tongue, meanwhile peeling her out of her garments as if he were peeling an orange. She had a magnificently flat stomach and a marvelous downy thatch at the junction of her legs. Her calves were well proportioned, her toes dainty, the nails painted an arousing red.

Her skin broke out in goosebumps as Fargo licked from her breasts to the soft base of her throat, and up along her neck to an ear. He inhaled a lobe and sucked awhile, then bestowed the same attention on the other one. Mabel was sensitive there, and she continually squirmed and opened and closed her legs while lavishing kisses and tiny bites on his chest and shoulders.

The bed creaked noisily when Fargo shifted his weight. He had to remember that when the time came, or they would make enough noise to bring Lucy on the run. He quivered as Mabel's mouth nibbled up his neck to his chin. Their lips fused, Mabel panting as if she had run a mile, her hands almost frantic as they roved everywhere except his groin. Whether she was shy or doing it on purpose was of no consequence. Fargo was still as hard as iron, his manhood throbbing with the need for release.

Fargo ran a hand through her hair, the hairs so soft and fine that running his fingers through them was akin to running them over satin. He massaged her neck, her shoulders. She did the same to his back and hips. The tip of his manhood was pressing against her thatch and he could feel the tremendous heat she was generating from her nether region.

Mabel's fingers plucked at Fargo's pants, and he took that as his cue to remove his boots and strip his pants off. Her palms slid sensually up and down his legs, always to within an inch of his manhood but never touching it. He lowered a hand to her knee, and she shook as if she had caught a chill, although that couldn't have been any farther from the truth. Ever so slowly, to heighten her suspense, Fargo traced his fingertips upward toward her fount of pleasure.

A sharp gasp escaped her. Mabel's eyes were hooded pools of pure lust, her cheeks tinged pink, her lips swollen with passion. Her bottom was moving to an internal rhythm, hunching forward as if to draw him into her.

Fargo's hand was almost to her molten slit. He had the illusion he was about to plunge it into a raging fire. Indeed, when he finally brushed a forefinger across it, she was burning hot. And soaking wet. Her inner thighs were drenched, a mere hint of the deluge yet to come.

Mabel rose off the bed, her eyelids fluttering, her mouth flung wide again. She didn't cry out, though. Her arms wrapped tight around his shoulders and she buried her lips against his neck, her body quaking from head to toe.

Fargo lightly stroked her swollen knob. Each touch provoked another ardent tremor, just as each pluck of a guitar string provoked a musical note. Her legs rose up around his hips.

"Please!" Mabel whispered. "Please!"

Fargo's forefinger slowly slid deeper into her tunnel. Soon it was buried to the knuckle. Her inner walls contracted and rippled around it, and her backside rose upward in a rocking motion. The bed started to creak again, and she stopped bucking and trembled instead, her burning body flush against his.

"I'm sorry," Mabel whispered. "I wish we did not have to be so damn quiet."

So did Fargo, but it couldn't be helped. Or could it? "Hold on to me," he whispered. When she did as he'd requested, he scooted her to the edge of the bed, lifted her body, and eased down onto the floorboards, lying on his back with her on top.

"I've never done it this way," Mabel cooed, sounding excited at the prospect.

"Just so the damn boards don't creak, too," Fargo said.

Mabel straddled him just below his member and leaned down over him, her breasts jiggling invitingly above his mouth. Fargo couldn't resist and clamped his lips to her right nipple. Her superbly smooth posterior occupied his hands. For her part, Mabel sighed and kept squeezing her thighs against his.

"I want you so badly."

Fargo believed her. Especially when Mabel suddenly grasped his member and raised herself above it, aligning her womanhood. With a swift downward plunge, she impaled herself to the hilt, her eyes widening, her nostrils flaring. For a few moments she was perfectly still, scarcely even breathing, then she began a rocking motion, forward and back, forward and back, her palms flat on his shoulders for added leverage.

Fargo relaxed and let her do most of the work. He kissed her melons, her neck, her arms. He fondled her sleek inner thighs, which were growing wetter by the moment.

"Oh!" Mabel said, then caught herself and bit her lower lip to keep from making the same mistake again.

The exquisite sensation also had an effect on Fargo. He began to rise up to meet her downward thrusts, matching his tempo to hers, their two bodies pumping in unison, a living piston in a carnal steam engine.

Mabel closed her eyes and thrust against him with heightened vigor and speed. She was still biting her lip, but small breathless sounds fluttered from her throat, and every now and again she would utter a low groan like the wind keening through trees.

Fargo hoped Lucy Brunsdale had fallen asleep. Otherwise, the maid might be in hot water. He couldn't stop, though, even if he were so inclined. His own passion had risen to a fever pitch. He had a constriction in his throat and another low down on his manhood, and it required every shred of willpower he possessed not to explode before he was ready.

"Yes!" Mabel whispered. "Yesssssss!"

Her hips were a blur. Fargo felt her spurt, felt his legs grow damp. She stiffened and was momentarily still, then slammed into him with a renewed vengeance, driving her bottom against him as if she were striving to pound him through the floor. The boards didn't creak, but the slap of their bodies was still much too loud, and Fargo held as still as he could to keep from adding to the noise.

Mabel threw back her head, her chest heaving, thrashing now as another wave of pleasure crashed over her.

Fargo gripped her hips to lock their bodies and heaved up into her. He was close to the pinnacle himself and it would not take much to send him over the edge. He was swollen, engorged, fit to explode.

Cooing softly, Mabel gave a delicate twist to her bottom, and it was all that was needed to bring on Fargo's release. He drove up into her, raising her off the floor, as undiluted bliss coursed through him and the bedroom swam into a white haze. Again and again he speared his pole in as deep as it would go. Gradually, he slowed. Not until he was totally spent did he stop and lay still, catching his breath.

Mabel sagged on top of him, her hair falling across his shoulders. For quite some time she shook ever-so-slightly, until she, too, lay quiet.

Fargo resisted an urge to doze off. Were he to fall asleep, he doubted he would wake up before morning, and they would have a heap of explaining to do if Lucy caught them together.

Marshaling his energy, he raised his head and whispered in the maid's ear, "Mabel? I should go." When she didn't answer, Fargo craned his neck to see her face. She was sound asleep, her lips fluttering with each breath, "Mabel?" he said a little louder, and gently shook her. She slept on, oblivious.

Sliding his arms under her limp body, Fargo slowly sat up. He rose, grunting from the strain, and braced her with one forearm while turning back the quilt. Then he carefully set her on the bed, her head on the pillow, and covered her to keep her warm.

Fumbling at his buckskins, Fargo dressed. His limbs were sluggish, his mind clogged by cobwebs. Exhaustion was taking its toll. Carrying his gunbelt, he silently opened her door and peeked down the hall. No one was abroad. The other doors were still shut. Sliding out, he closed hers and was in his own bedroom on his own bed within seconds.

Undressing seemed like too much of a chore. Fargo tossed his hat aside and wearily sank onto his back. The instant he closed his eyes, he was asleep, adrift in slumber so deep he did something he rarely did; he overslept. Ordinarily, out of habit, he was invariably up at the crack of dawn. But when he struggled out of dreamland into the bright light of morning, he could tell by the sparkling shafts of sunshine streaming through the window that it was well past dawn. Eight, or possibly later.

Fargo swung his legs over the side of the bed and shook his head to clear it. Someone had entered while he slept and left a wash bowl and a pitcher filled with water on the small stand by the head of the bed. Beside them were a folded cloth and towel. He quickly washed up, strapped on the Colt, donned his hat, and strode out to greet the new day.

The door to Luther's room was closed and no sounds came from within. No one was in the dining room. No one was in the parlor. Either most everyone else was still in bed, or they had gone out. Fargo was about to go to Mabel's room and see if she was around when he noticed the wall clock read five minutes to nine. Five minutes until he was to meet with the Hanken clan.

Brilliant sunlight near blinded him when Fargo opened the front door. Squinting, he stepped outside.

"Nice to see you're punctual, friend."

Seth and his sons were lounging next to the building, Orville and Theodore stretched out with blades of grass stuck between their teeth, Harry whittling on a piece of wood, Josiah doodling in the dirt with a finger.

The line camp was as unnaturally lifeless as the house. Oxen stood idle. Equipment went unused. Only a few loggers were about, dashing from building to building or tent to tent with anxious glances at the foreboding forest hemming the encampment.

"So what is it you wanted to talk to us about?" Seth asked. "Going after Phantoms, I hope. My boys and me are raring to make them pay for Bobby."

Fargo hunkered and motioned for them to huddle around. He detailed what he had learned and how he proposed to deal with the Phantoms, and when he was done, the Hankens were rooted in stunned amazement until Seth uttered a low snarl.

"If what you've just told us is true, I won't rest until every last one of the bastards is six feet under."

"How many of them do you reckon there are?" Orville asked.

"It's hard to say," Fargo confessed. "I shot one. My best guess would be eight or nine. No more than that, or it would be hard for them to keep it a secret."

"You're taking an awful chance," Seth said. "We'll do as you want, but if we slip up, your life won't be worth a hill of beans. Yours, and Mr. Brunsdale's, both."

"I know you won't let me down," Fargo stated.

Seth was touched by the sentiment and clasped Fargo's hand in both of his. "Mister, you've got yourself a friend for life. You can count on us to be there when you need us. Right, boys?"

All four sons bobbed their heads, and Harry said, "Damn right we will, Pa. Those polecats have hell to pay for what they did to Bobby."

Fired with a zeal for vengeance, the Hankens drifted off past the cookhouse. Fargo's stomach rumbled at the thought of food. Rising, he walked around the house to check on the Ovaro. The stallion was right where he had left it, contentedly grazing. So were his saddle and saddle blanket. He turned to go and saw four men striding toward him.

In the lead was the bull of the woods, Rem Dinsmore, his ham-sized fists balled in anger. Two of the men with him were loggers Fargo had never set eyes on before. The last one was none other than Modoc Jim.

"I want a word with you," the foreman announced.

"Maybe I don't want one with you," Fargo said, and started toward the corner, only to have his path blocked by the pair of husky timbermen. Modoc Jim stayed well back, his rifle in the crook of an elbow.

"That's too bad," Dinsmore said, planting himself. "We're having this out here and now whether you like it or not."

"Having what out?" Fargo stalled. It looked as if he were in for it. No one else was anywhere around, and he couldn't reach the back door before they reached him.

"Don't play dumb. I don't want you hanging around Lucy. She's mine, and mine alone, and I'll gladly break the back of anyone who thinks different." Dinsmore smacked his left fist into his right palm.

"Does that include Lucy?"

The big logger glowered. "What are you babbling about?"

"She told me that she doesn't want anything more to do with you," Fargo said. "So I guess you'll have to break her back to set her straight. Do it when she's not looking. Sneak up behind her so she can't defend herself." Fargo glanced at the Modoc. "Or maybe have your friend, there, shoot her from ambush. He's good at that, isn't he?"

"Keep Modoc Jim out of this. It doesn't concern him."

"Doesn't it?" Fargo responded. "He's involved. Along with Cleve Sneldon and Grizwald and Oddie—" Stopping, Fargo snapped his fingers, "Wait. I forgot. Oddie's dead. I shot him down at the notch yesterday."

"This isn't about the other thing. This is about Lucy," Dinsmore growled.

"It's all related, although I didn't catch on at first," Fargo said. "The Phantoms, you, Sykes and Walter, Cleve Sneldon. Admit it."

Dinsmore took a step, his shoulders hunched, his cheeks puffing outward, a mad bull about to charge. "I admit nothing. Quit trying to put words in my mouth. Lucy is the issue, nothing else." He jabbed a thick thumb at the pinto. "I want you to saddle up and ride out right this minute."

"Don't I get to say good-bye to the Brunsdales?"

"Don't push me. You're lucky I'm allowing you to leave with all your teeth." Dinsmore took another step. "Now get on your damn horse."

"I'd rather it were my idea," Fargo said, and hit the bigger man flush on the jaw, a powerful uppercut that jarred Rem Dinsmore backward. The pair of hefty lumbermen leaped to help but were stopped by a snarl from the foreman.

"Stay out of this! He's mine, all mine! Anyone who interferes will regret it." Dinsmore rubbed his chin, then sneered, 'Not bad. I can't recollect the last time someone hit me that hard."

"There's plenty more where that came from," Fargo said, raising both fists chest high. "Unless you have more sense than I credit you with."

"I'm not as stupid as you think," Dinsmore said, and launched himself forward with both huge arms flailing, raining punches in a ceaseless battering barrage, relying on his greater bulk to end their fight before it really began.

Fargo sidestepped and landed a blow to the kidney that made Dinsmore bellow in rage. A backhand to the face nearly took Fargo's head off but he ducked and flicked several swift jabs to the ribs, then skipped back out of reach before Dinsmore could retaliate.

"Was that supposed to hurt?" the foreman mocked him.

"Not as much as this," Fargo answered, and darted in close to slam a right cross to the logger's jaw. Dinsmore rocked, steadied himself, and swung a looping left that only clipped Fargo's temple but still knocked him rearward half a dozen feet with fireflies pinwheeling in front of his eyes.

"I can keep at this all day if I have to," the bruiser declared, "Do yourself a favor and do as I told you."

"I'm staying," Fargo vowed.

"Think again."

Fargo's vision cleared just as a two-legged train slammed into him. Dinsmore's shoulder smashed into his gut and he was lifted off his feet, the man's immense arms around his torso. His breath whooshed from his lungs and he was sucked into a vortex of dizziness and fleeting nausea. The next he knew, he crashed to earth and gruff laughter rang in his ears.

"He sure is a tough one, Rem," one of the timbermen said.

"My sister could beat him with one arm tied behind her back," hooted the other.

Iron fingers seized Fargo by the shirt and jerked him a few inches off the ground as Dinsmore's face floated into view.

"You had your chance. Now I'm going to wallop the tar out of you. Then we'll saddle your nag ourselves, throw you over him, and escort you out of camp."

Fargo was pushed back down. He saw a stout leg rise above him and a boot poised to stomp. Lunging upward, he grabbed hold of Dinsmore's ankle and wrenched, throwing all of his weight into it. Caught by surprise, Rem Dinsmore yelped, tottered, and fell onto his hands and knees.

Heaving upright, Fargo let the foreman start to rise. Then he delivered a searing combination to the cheek and ear. Almost any other adversary would have buckled, but all it did was make Rem Dinsmore mad.

Snorting and swearing, the bull of the woods lived up to his nickname. He surged upward as if slung by a slingshot, his great arms outspread, his fingers clawed to seize and rend. But Fargo was quicker, and evaded him. Madder than ever, Dinsmore hurtled forward, and this time he succeeded in clamping both arms around Fargo's chest.

"I'll crush you like an eggshell!"

The man was full of threats, but this one might come true. Struggling fiercely, Fargo sought to break free. A losing proposition, for no matter what he did, no matter how hard he fought, Dinsmore's arms constricted tighter and tighter. Pain spiked his rib cage, and he could feel his ribs slowly but inexorably caving in under the titanic pressure.

Rem Dinsmore laughed. He was enjoying himself, enjoying himself immensely. He thrived on inflicting pain and punishment.

Taking a deep breath, Fargo expanded his chest, seeking to loosen the foreman's hold enough to slip loose. But Dinsmore merely wrapped his arms tighter and laughed in his face.

"You don't have a prayer."

Fargo begged to differ. Whipping his head back, he drove his forehead into the bigger man's nose. Cartilage crunched and blood spurted, and Rem Dinsmore howled like a stricken wolf. The pressure slackened, enabling Fargo to press both hands against the foreman's midsection and push with all his might. He tumbled from the other's grasp, landed on his shoulder, and rolled up into a crouch.

Dinsmore hadn't moved. Scarlet splashed his face, and he was holding a hand over his ravaged nose. "You broke it!" he thundered.

"You're so ugly no one will notice," Fargo said to rile him, and the ruse worked,

Roaring like a grizzly, Dinsmore pounced. There was no method to his attack, no skill, no finesse. He lumbered in with his fists upraised and left himself wide open.

Fargo launched himself upward, his own fist streaking from ground level up into Dinsmore's chin with a resounding crack. It was unlikely the foreman realized what had hit him. Staggering drunkenly, he blinked a few times, spittle dribbling over his lower lip. Fargo had the advantage and he intended to keep it. He unleashed a flurry of hooks, jabs, crosses, and straight punches, battering Dinsmore mercilessly, pounding him again and again, hammering him again and again. Dinsmore blocked a few of the blows, but the majority connected. And no matter how big a man was, or how strong, if enough blows scored, eventually they would wear him down and bring him to his knees.

When Fargo stepped back, that's exactly where the foreman was, swaying groggily, his face a red ruin. The other two loggers were too stupefied by the outcome to intervene. Modoc Jim's bronzed face was as emotionless as a blank slate.

"From here on out, you will leave Lucy Brunsdale alone," Fargo said.

Weakly swiping at the blood pouring from his nose and mouth, Dinsmore rasped, "Like hell I will."

A solid right cross flattened Rem Dinsmore on the spot. Still conscious, he clawed at the dirt, seeking to rise.

Fargo lowered his arms and turned to the Modoc, his hand brushing the butt of his Colt. He would like to settle things then and there, but if he gunned the Modoc down without being able to show cause, they would accuse him of murder. "How about you? Care to start something?"

The Modoc was too smart to try. His cold eyes stared flatly.

"Well, well. What have we here?" Addison Sykes and Walter Brunsdale were at the corner of the building, Walter picking his teeth with a gold toothpick, Addison frowning down at Rem Dinsmore. "Is it traditional at logging camps to start the day with a bout of fisticuffs?"

"We had a slight disagreement over Lucy Brunsdale," Fargo said.

"Did you, indeed?" Addison's frown deepened and he stepped over to nudge the foreman with the toe of his polished shoe. "It seems some people never learn. And after all those talks we had on the subject."

Fargo decided to put his plan into motion. "Have either of you seen Cleve Sneldon? He has a lot to answer for."

Walter removed the toothpick from his mouth long enough to ask, "And what might that be?"

"I saw him signaling with a mirror to someone yesterday.

I suspect he's been secretly working with the Phantoms all this time."

Addison chortled. "That timid little mouse? In league with a pack of savages? Don't be ridiculous."

"I never claimed the Phantoms were Indians," Fargo said. "The fact is, they're not. Except for one of them." He deliberately looked right at Modoc Jim.

"These are remarkable accusations you're making," Addison said gravely. "I trust you have adequate proof to back them up? Proof that would suffice in a court of law?"

"Not yet, but I will soon," Fargo dangled the bait he hoped they wouldn't be able to resist. "By this evening at the latest. And I won't bother with the courts. I'll call a meeting of all the loggers and tell them what has been happening. They'll do the rest."

"Why, the roughnecks would lynch the Phantoms outright!" Walter Brunsdale blurted.

Fargo nodded. "And let them hang there to rot." He walked off without a backward glance. For better or worse he had done it. He had stuck his head in a snare. Now the rest was up to the Phantoms. Either he would expose them for who they really were, or they would kill him.

It was that simple.

12

Skye Fargo spent the rest of the morning waiting for the axe to drop. The next move was up to the Phantoms, and only they knew when they would strike. Or how. Would it be a bullet to the back? He wondered. Or would they jump him when they thought he was least likely to expect it? He was always on his guard, always alert, but the tension gnawed at his nerves as he stalked the line camp making a target of himself.

After his tussle with the bull of the woods, Fargo strolled to the near-empty cookhouse and was treated to a late break-fast by the friendly cook. The loggers had already eaten their morning meal and the cook was hard at work preparing the next, but he stopped to rustle up a heaping helping of eggs and bacon. "My way of thanking you, mister, for helping Mr. Brunsdale like I've heard you done," was how the cook put it as he brought over the plate.

Fargo washed the food down with five cups of coffee thickened with spoonfuls of sugar. Whenever he was on the trail, he had to settle for having his coffee black since he always traveled light. But now he indulged his sweet tooth, and then some, since it might well be the last coffee he ever drank.

When Fargo ambled from the cookhouse half an hour later, dozens of loggers were out and about. It had been over twenty-four hours since the sniper last struck, and camp life was returning to normal.

Rem Dinsmore had begun organizing work parties, He glared at Fargo as Fargo went by, his face swollen and discolored from the severe beating he had taken. It had worsened his normally sour disposition, and he was a terror as he roared among the men, barking orders like a general gone amok.

By noon the camp was almost deserted. Fallers had been sent to fell trees, buckers to saw larger trees into workable sections, choker setters to prepare the trees for hauling, bull whackers to handle the yokes of oxen that did the actual hauling, skid greasers to keep the skids greased, and flume herders to ensure the chute did not become jammed.

Fargo walked around the camp for another hour, making it as easy for the Phantoms as he could, but nothing happened. He began to think they were too smart to fall for his ruse, and he bent his steps toward the main house to check on Luther. He had not seen Lucy or Mabel all morning, and figured they were tending the timber baron.

Except for the loud ticking of the wall clock, a hush lay over the house. Fargo walked down the hall to Luther's room. The door was closed, and he rapped lightly so as not to awaken Luther if he were asleep.

"Come in, Mr. Fargo. We have been expecting you."

Fargo's hand dropped to his Colt. Wary of a trap, he slowly pushed on the door. Addison Sykes and Walter Brunsdale were seated in chairs by an empty bed, as smug and self-assured as ever. By the window stood Cleve Sneldon, nervously wringing his hands.

"Where's Luther and the women?" Fargo demanded.

"All in good time," Walter glibly responded. "If you're through parading around the camp in the futile hope we would be stupid enough to give ourselves away, perhaps we can bring this affair to a suitable conclusion." His smug grin widened. "Although not quite in the fashion you conceived."

None of them appeared to be armed, but Fargo jerked the Colt out anyway and trained it on Sykes. "If you've hurt them, you're a dead man,"

"Oh, please," Addison said. "Melodramatics are beneath you. You're in no position to threaten us and you know it. Hand your revolver to Mr. Sneldon."

"And if I don't?" Fargo said.

Irritation brought Addison out of his chair. "Must I spell it out for you? Cooperate, and we will take you to where they are. Refuse, and you will never see them again."

"How do I know they're not already dead?"

Walter also stood. "You don't. But we couldn't very well kill them and smuggle their bodies out of camp, now could we? They rode out with a few of our men half an hour ago. Lucy was fuming, but she went along as peacefully as a kitten out of fear for her father's well-being."

"We had to wait until the camp was clear of loggers to confront you," Addison mentioned. "A prudent precaution on our part, wouldn't you say?" He gestured impatiently. "The revolver, if you please."

Fargo pretended to hesitate. They might suspect he was up to something if he were to seem too eager. "All right. You win," he said, reversing his grip and extending the Colt toward the secretary.

Sneldon edged around the chairs to take it, then quickly stepped back as if afraid he would be jumped.

"Of course we do," Walter bragged. "We always have, we always will. We win because we let no one stand in our way. When we want something, we remove every obstacle to achieving our goal."

"Even your own nephew and his daughter," Fargo said.

Addison walked to the doorway. "Spare us your scorn. We bent over backward to give Luther every opportunity to see things our way. His shortsighted insistence on always striving to live up to his scruples was his downfall. The fault is his, not ours."

"You honestly believe that, don't you?" Fargo could not remember meeting two people he loathed more.

"The ends always justify the means," Addison said. "To be a captain of industry, a man must be willing to sacrifice

146

a few of his soldiers and eliminate anyone who opposes him," He gestured toward the rear. "Out the back, if you please. Our horses are waiting. As soon as you saddle yours, we can go."

No one was in sight. Fargo was mounted within minutes. The three conspirators led him northward, keeping to the rear of the buildings where they were less apt to be seen by the few loggers still in camp. Once they were screened by the trees, they trotted to the flume and followed it eastward for a quarter of a mile to a clearing where over a dozen horses were tethered. From thirty feet above came the hiss of water and the rumble of logs being sent down the chute to the mill at the base of the cascade.

Fargo drew rein at the clearing's edge. Luther lay on a blanket on the ground, Lucy and Mabel beside him. All three looked up at him in despair, Lucy with tears brimming her eyes.

"See? I told you they were alive," Addison said.

Hovering near Lucy was Rem Dinsmore. Modoc Jim was there, a rifle in one hand, a bow and a quiver of arrows slung across his back. Grizwald was sharpening a knife. Eight other loggers were standing around awaiting orders.

"The Phantoms," Fargo said.

"*Our* Phantoms, to be precise," Addison said. "Quite ingenious, don't you think? All those loggers out beating the bush after a tribe of nonexistent savages, when the whole time the ones they were after were right under their very noses." He motioned. "After you."

Fargo rode over to the Brunsdales and the maid, and dismounted. Instantly, Rem Dinsmore bunched his huge fists and came toward him, but the foreman halted at a rebuke from Sykes.

"That will be far enough, Rem! He has already pounded you into the dirt once today, and I, for one, do not care to see the pitiful spectacle repeated. I should think you wouldn't, either." Addison climbed down, hooked his thumbs in his vest, and strutted forward like a rooster. "This is a great moment.

After all these months, our plotting has borne fruit. By this time tomorrow Walter and I will be the sole heads of the Syndicate, Cleve will be the new manager, and we can start clear-cutting the forests."

Walter alighted, and chuckled. "Glorious. Simply glorious. At last it is all about to pay off."

Luther rose onto his elbows, gritting his teeth against the pain. Perspiration dotted his brow and there were dark bags under his eyes. "I don't understand any of this, Uncle. Why go to such extremes? Why didn't you simply vote me out as a partner long ago? Why did so many of my men have to die?"

Addison made a clucking noise and sadly shook his head. "Your stupidity is as pathetic as Dinsmore's. We concocted the idea of a lost tribe to ultimately have someone to blame for your death."

Walter nodded. "Consider the lengths we've gone to as a credit to the influence you wield." When he saw that Luther still did not comprehend, Walter squatted and folded his hands on his knees. "We realized almost a year ago, nephew, that you would never accept our plans for the Syndicate. We discussed voting you out as a partner, but there was a potential problem. You're a close friend of the governor's and other important people. We were concerned you might use your influence to make things hard for us."

Addison took up the account. "We certainly didn't want the state government at our throats. We considered hiring an assassin to dispose of you, but there was bound to be an official inquiry."

"We needed you out of the way," Walter resumed, "but it either had to look like an accident, or be blamed on someone else. One night over lobster we came up with the idea of blaming it on Indians. Savages kill whites all the time and no one gives it a second thought."

Luther was horrorstruck. "You went to all this trouble on my account? You killed all those innocent people?"

"Millions of dollars were at stake," Walter said. "We had

to arrange things so your friends in high office and your own men would accept your death without question."

Addison laughed. "You are so naive, Luther. You never caught on that the loggers being killed were the men who were most loyal to you."

Lucy began to rise, her whole body quivering with outrage, and Fargo grabbed her wrist. "You are monsters!" she railed at the partners. "Inhuman monsters!"

"And soon we'll be inhumanly *rich* monsters," Addison joked.

Walter straightened. "Not that our enterprise hasn't suffered its share of setbacks. Sumersby's death was an accident. He was supposed to manage the mill for us, but now Mr. Sneldon has agreed to fill in for a substantial increase in the amount we've already paid him."

Luther glanced at his secretary. "Cleve?"

"Don't look so shocked," Walter said. "We needed a spy, someone who could keep an eye on you. He was the one who informed us Mr. Dinsmore was unhappy with the status quo and could also be bought for the right price."

Their betrayals plainly cut Luther to his core. "I trusted both of you," he said, crestfallen. "I paid you more than fair salaries. I treated you decently."

Rem Dinsmore snorted. "Oh, you treated me decently enough, except when it came to your daughter. You knew how much I loved her, how I wanted her for my wife. I begged you to talk to her on my behalf but you refused."

"She's a grown woman. She makes her own decisions," Luther responded.

Fargo felt Lucy's arm tense up and he grabbed her other wrist to keep her from springing at the foreman. It was important he keep the three of them close to him. It would not be long before all hell broke loose.

"You expected me to marry *you*?" Lucy virtually screeched. "You rotten traitor! You've had your own men killed! You've stabbed my father in the back! And now you're going to stand

149

there and let them murder the three of us, not lift a finger to help."

Dinsmore shook his head. "No, not the three of you. Just your father and Mabel. They promised me you wouldn't come to any harm." He glanced at Sykes and Walter. "Isn't that right? Tell her."

Addison pursed his lips and took his time answering. "Well, you see, Mr. Dinsmore, we haven't been entirely honest with you. The simple fact is we can't leave witnesses. The rest of these men have been bought off, and we can count on Modoc Jim,"—he nodded at the Modoc, who reached back over his shoulder—"to them to keep quiet. Miss Brunsdale is another matter."

"You gave your word," Rem said.

"And you believed them?" Fargo interrupted while scanning the undergrowth for telltale movement. "They've been using you to get what you want, just like they've used everyone else."

Dinsmore stepped between Lucy and Sykes. "I won't let you harm her. You know how much she means to me."

"Ah, yes. Love is grand," Addison said, his tone dripping with acid. "But your fondness for Miss Brunsdale is of no consequence whatsoever. Your loyalty to us, however, is. So the question boils down to this. Will you side with the Syndicate or cast your lot with her?"

Rem glanced from Sykes to Walter. "How can you treat me like this? I've worked hard to do everything you asked of me. I bribed men I knew we could trust. I hired the Modoc. I laid ambushes for my own crews. And this is how you repay me?" The foreman thrust a calloused hand at Lucy. "Come on. I'm getting you out of here. We'll head for Mexico, just as I planned all along. You're mad at me now, but after a while you'll grow to care for me as much as I care for you,"

Addison let out an exaggerated sigh and said to Walter Brunsdale, "Do you suppose it's something in the water? Stupidity is simply running rampant." He smiled at Dinsmore. "I'm afraid you have just become expendable."

"Try anything and I'll snap your spine in half," the fore-man snarled.

"Like this?" Addison said, and snapped his fingers.

An arrow thumped into Rem Dinsmore's wide back be-tween his shoulder blades. The impact drove him almost to his knees but he recovered his balance and twisted toward Modoc Jim, who had knocked another shaft to the sinew bow-string with lightning speed. "Bastard!" Dinsmore spat, and lumbered toward the killer with his great hands hooked to break and rend. A second shaft caught him in the center of the chest and he oozed to the grass, his gaze fixing on Lucy Brunsdale as he died.

Cleve Sneldon looked fit to be ill. "Did you have to do that, Mr. Sykes?" he squeaked.

"You heard him," Addison said. "He was a threat to the Syndicate, and anyone who is a threat must be eliminated." Sykes nonchalantly draped his forearm over the secretary's scrawny shoulder. "If you're going to be of value to us, Cleve, you must learn to get over this squeamishness of yours."

"Maybe I should forget about managing the mill," Snel-don said. "Maybe I should just take my money and head for New York as I originally intended." He absently placed his hand on the butt of Fargo's revolver, which was wedged under his belt.

Off in the pines a lanky form darted from one trunk to another. Only Fargo saw it, and he inwardly smiled, then leaned toward Lucy. "Help has arrived," he whispered in her ear. "When the shooting starts, hit the ground and stay there. I don't want you taking a slug by mistake."

Walter Brunsdale faced Sneldon. "We would be most dis-pleased if you deserted us in our time of need, Cleve."

Fargo bent down and whispered the same instructions to Mabel. He didn't think anyone was paying attention to them but Addison Sykes suddenly glanced around sharply.

"What are you up to, Mr. Fargo? There will be no talk-ing unless I say you can talk."

Other figures were converging on the clearing. Fleet as deer, and silent as panthers, they snuck to within a dozen yards of the unsuspecting Phantoms and crouched or knelt to bring their Kentucky rifles to bear. Seth Hanken touched his right hand to his cheek, the prearranged signal for when his sons were in position.

Modoc Jim, Fargo saw, had notched yet another arrow and was pointing it at him. He slowly held his hands out from his sides to convince the cutthroats he had no intention of causing trouble. "I have a question I'd like to ask," he said.

"Be our guest," Walter graciously consented. "A last request for the condemned, if you will. What is it you would like to know?"

"If the two of you would be willing to turn yourselves in to the law."

The Syndicate bigwigs blinked, then howled with glee, Addison smacking his leg as if it were the funniest joke he had ever heard. A lot of the Phantoms joined in. The Modoc, though, was as devoid of humor as he was of emotion and continued to hold the bow and arrow rock steady.

"Amazing, simply amazing," Addison Sykes said when his mirth subsided. "Here you are on the verge of oblivion and you make light of it. And to answer your question, no, we would never admit to our guilt. Even if we were caught dead to rights, we would deny everything and hire a battery of lawyers to get us out of prison."

"That's why we keep some of the best lawyers money can buy on retainer," Walter said. "'And if they should fail, we know of judges who are not above being bribed to commute a sentence."

"With our wealth and influence there is no way in hell we would ever spend time behind bars," Addison crowed.

Fargo slowly nodded. "I figured as much. Then I guess the only way to stop you is to kill you."

Walter sobered and raked him up and down with a probing scrutiny. "How, exactly, do you propose to do that when you're outnumbered thirteen to one?"

"Thirteen to six," Fargo corrected him, and touched his hand to his right cheek.

Five Kentucky rifles boomed simultaneously. At the thunder of their combined blasts, five Phantoms dropped where they stood. Four were loggers. The fifth was Modoc Jim, the most dangerous of the bunch, the man Fargo had told the Hankens they must be sure to slay with their first volley.

Grizwald and the surviving Phantoms swung toward the woods and opened fire at random, wildly peppering the underbrush. Addison Sykes crouched low, pulling Walter down with him, but Cleve Sneldon gawked in fright at the encircling foliage, then whirled to flee.

Lucy and Mabel had done as Fargo directed and were hugging the ground, Lucy shielding her father with her own body.

For his part, Fargo had also dropped down, but when Sneldon spun to run off, he took two long strides and tackled him. Fargo grabbed for the Colt, but the secretary shifted and tried to knee him in the groin. A twist of his hips deflected the blow. Grappling, they rolled back and forth, Sneldon exhibiting surprising strength.

Around them the battle raged. The Hankens had reloaded and unleashed another volley, while the Phantoms were firing as fast as they could squeeze the trigger. The din was almost deafening.

Slamming his left fist into Sneldon's jaw, Fargo palmed the Colt and rose onto his left knee. He snapped a shot at a nearby logger, who toppled with a third hole above his nostrils.

Cleve Sneldon had gone momentarily limp, but now he heaved erect and bolted toward the forest. He did not get very far. A stray slug knocked him sideways. Tottering, he clutched at his side, and when he brought his hand away, it was covered with blood. He stumbled several more feet, his mouth opening and closing like that of a fish out of water, then he collapsed, his dream of one day visiting New York dying with him.

Acrid clouds of stinging gunsmoke shrouded the clearing.

Fargo glimpsed the women and Luther, all of them still prone, and still alive. Nearby lay Walter Brunsdale, half of his face blown away.

Fargo glanced at the spot where Modoc Jim had fallen and was startled to see the killer was gone. Tucking at the knees, he ran toward the south end of the clearing and spied the Modoc and Addison Sykes darting into the woods bordering the flume. He gave chase. Just then he glanced over a shoulder and his rifle leaped up, spitting lead and flame.

Flinging himself flat, Fargo heard the slug whine overhead. In a twinkling he was up and running, resolved to pursue them all the way to the Willamette Valley if he had to. One way or another, he was going to finally end the bloodshed.

The Modoc had an elbow pressed to his ribs and he was slightly doubled over, but he was moving more swiftly than most men could ever hope to. Addison Sykes was hard pressed to keep up. Too much easy living had taken a toll.

Fargo had an unobstructed shot at Sykes's broad back but he didn't take it. Backshooting was for dry gulchers. Soon he began to gain on the pair, but again he had to seek cover when Modoc Jim levered two shots at him. He whipped up the Colt, only to have Addison Sykes blunder into the sights, huffing and puffing like a bull on its last legs.

Modoc Jim angled toward the open ground under the flume where they could go faster. He pulled ahead of Sykes, who called out for him to slow down. The renegade ignored the command,

Fargo hurtled from the vegetation, eager for one clear shot at Modoc Jim. He took a bead and was going to shout the Modoc's name when Addison Sykes halted, turned, and threw his arms into the air, blocking Fargo's view.

"Don't shoot! I give up! I give up!"

Fargo stepped to one side in time to catch sight of the wily warrior disappearing into the woods. Wishing Seth or one of Seth's boys were there to take care of Sykes, he advanced. Almost too late, the gleam of metal in Sykes's hand caused him to dive to the left at the very instant a derringer cracked. Dirt kicked into his face. He thumbed off an answering shot, and Addison Sykes lurched but did not go down. The derringer cracked a second time. Fargo fanned the Colt, then rose, hastily replacing the cartridges.

The man who had been the cause of all the death and suffering was on his back, holes in his silk shirt where the designer had not intended. He attempted to sit up but his life was ebbing rapidly. "Not like this," he said to the sky. "A man of my stature. Not like this!" And just like that he died, his last breath a gurgling whine that matched the gurgling of the water in the flume above.

Fargo ran into the woods, scouring the woodland ahead for Modoc Jim. The killer had vanished, and that made him doubly dangerous. The Modoc could be anywhere, could strike at any moment.

A low limb gave Fargo an idea. Shoving the Colt into his holster, he stepped underneath it and jumped. Snagging hold, he hoisted himself high enough to lock his elbows, then scanned the forest in all directions. The gunfire had stopped. He spotted Seth and Orville in the clearing talking to Lucy, Luther and Mabel. The other Hankens—Harry, Josiah, and Theodore—were gathering up weapons from slain Phantoms.

Gazing westward again, Fargo tensed. Fifty yards away Modoc Jim had broken from cover and was streaking across the open ground below the flume. Letting go, Fargo dropped and was off like a shot, veering through the trees to intercept him. He thought the Modoc would pass under the flume and into the woods on the other side, but when he burst into the open, he was astounded to see Modoc Jim clambering up the trestle toward the chute. The killer's bow and quiver lay at the bottom, the rifle was slung across his back.

Fargo sprinted to the trestle, unlimbering the Colt. Modoc Jim spotted him, and turned. The whole front of the Modoc's shirt was bright crimson and soaked through and through. The killer was severely, perhaps fatally, wounded.

Fargo started up, climbing from one crossbeam to the next.

Modoc Jim reached the chute, hooked an elbow over the top, and slid over the rim, out of sight. Fargo had no idea what the renegade hoped to accomplish.

Imitating his quarry, Fargo forked an arm over the chute and pulled his head and shoulders above the rim. Swiftly flowing water filled two-thirds of the trough. Fifteen yards away Modoc Jim clung to the side and gazed intently up the mountain.

Fargo looked, and suddenly he understood.

The Modoc was weak from loss of blood, and knew he couldn't possibly escape on foot. So in desperation he had scaled the flume to try the impossible, to attempt to grab hold of a log as it swept past and ride it down to the bottom. The idea was insane. Logs reached speeds of eighty to ninety miles an hour and could crush anything in their path.

Another rumble heralded another log, a huge Douglas fir over a hundred feet long and five or six feet in diameter. It hurtled toward them at blinding speed, and within seconds the front end flashed past Fargo. He saw Modoc Jim coil and then leap outward to catch the leading edge with outstretched fingers. But the killer slipped as he jumped, and before he could throw himself out of harm's way, the giant log smashed into him with a horrendous crunch. The fir seemed to hop out of the water, then settled back again with a grinding shudder. In seconds it had swept on down the flume, on around the bend, and was gone.

Fargo stared at the mangled, pulped remains a moment. Hearing his name called, he saw Mabel and Seth hurrying toward him. With weary care, he lowered himself onto a crossbeam and descended.

"Is it over?" the old Tennessean asked.

"It's over," Fargo confirmed.

"We did just like you said. We hid out behind the cook-house and followed when you rode off," Seth chuckled. "Every last one of those polecats is dead. My Bobby can rest easier in his grave thanks to you." He clapped Fargo on the arm, and turned. "I just came to see how you were. Now I've got to get back. Miss Lucy wants my boys and me to help get her pa down to town for proper doctorin'." He hastened off.

Mabel rimmed her rosy lips with the tip of her tongue. "What about you, handsome? Care to stick around a while? It might be well worth your while."

Skye Fargo admired the swell of her bosom, and grinned. "Show me."

LOOKING FORWARD!
The following is the opening
section from the next novel in the exciting
Trailsman **series from Signet:**

THE TRAILSMAN #233
MISSOURI MAYHEM

Western Missouri, 1861—near the small town
of Plainview, where the men lived hard and
the women even harder, and where
turning your back on your kin
could earn you a deadly bullet.

"Mr. Fargo, they need you over at the office right now. Train got robbed and the Express car blown up about a half hour ago."

Fargo trotted to the railroad station and into the district manager's office. There were ten people there waiting for him.

Neville looked up, patted his balding head with a linen handkerchief. "Fargo, about time you got here. This is what came over the wire twenty-five minutes ago." He handed Fargo a yellow paper with hand printing.

ENGINE 460 WESTBOUND OUT OF ST. LOUIS ROBBED BY TWO ARMED MEN NEAR THE EIGHTY-SEVENTH MARKER AT 9:40 A.M. TODAY. EXPRESS CAR BLOWN OPEN, SAFE BLASTED AND EMPTIED. EXPRESS MAN KILLED, CONDUCTOR WOUNDED. TRAIN CONTINUING WESTWARD AT 9:54. NOW DUE IN PLAINVIEW, ESTIMATED 10:42 A.M.

Fargo dropped the paper and frowned. "How far is mile marker eighty-seven from here?"

"It's about twenty-six miles to the east," someone said.

"How soon do you have an eastbound train? Repair, work, freight, anything?"

Neville looked at the dispatcher. "Wilbur?"

"We have a switch engine and two work cars leaving here eastbound as soon as the string that was robbed gets here. Looks to be about ten forty-five. Depending on old Engine Four-Sixty."

"Hook up a cattle car so I can load on my horse. I'll need cleat boards for getting out. Let me off at mile marker eighty-seven. First I'll want to talk to the wounded conductor." Fargo looked at the new pocket watch he had bought. Since he was going to be in town for a while, he had figured he might need one. Townies tended to use the clock a lot. "That leaves me twenty-eight minutes to saddle my Ovaro and get on board." He turned to leave.

"Mr. Fargo," Neville said. "These filthy robbers killed one of our own and wounded a conductor. I want those killers. Make sure you bring them in dead or alive."

Fargo nodded and hurried out of the office.

At the livery stable he found the Ovaro in the small pasture behind the stable. He whistled, and the black and white pinto pricked up his ears, turned, and trotted over to the gate. Fargo rubbed the big animal's ears and patted his neck. The pinto's fore- and hindquarters were jet black and the midsection creamy white.

It took Fargo five minutes to comb down the pinto and saddle him. His saddlebags carried a supply of beef jerky. He filled a two-quart flat canteen and tied it on, then rode the Ovaro down the street to the depot and up on the freight platform. After tying the Ovaro to a luggage cart, Fargo sat down and waited.

Fifteen minutes later, a train came rolling in. The engine number was 460. Two dozen train men and townsmen, including the doctor, were there. They took the conductor off first and put him in a wheelchair. Neville talked to him, then Fargo had his turn.

"Can you describe the killers?"

"Oh, yes. Never forget them. One was tall, young, and red-headed. Said his name was Plimpton. Second man was a head shorter and had a paunch. Wore a brown cowboy hat and tied-down six-gun."

"That's enough," Dr. Andrews said. "I need this man in my office to tend to his leg." He waved, and a man pushed the chair away toward the town side of the tracks. Fargo went back to where he had left the pinto on the freight platform.

As soon as the 460 train headed west, a work string came on the main line and pulled up to the platform with an added boxcar with the big door open. The pinto had no problem going into the dark hole of the boxcar. He'd been on many like it before. Fargo dismounted, tied the reins to a bar on the side of the car, and welcomed the bale of hay that a freight handler rolled up on a hand truck. Fargo sat on the hay, leaned against the far side of the boxcar, and had a perfect window on this part of Missouri out the open door for the next twenty-six miles.

Fargo figured the robbers must have jumped off the train while it was still moving. Otherwise, the passengers and trainmen would have seen them. It wouldn't be hard to find where two men had jumped and rolled off a rail car. They must have carried or thrown off their loot in heavy bags or maybe even mail sacks. Fargo decided to start his search a quarter mile before the mile marker and continue for a half mile past it.

At a steady thirty-five miles an hour the work engine jolted the short train to the east. They would hit the eighty-seven-mile marker in about forty-five minutes. Skye watched the fertile countryside flash by. Lots of farms and small towns were starting to emerge. In a hundred years this would be solid farms and towns and maybe even cities. It would be interesting to come back in a century and look at all the changes, Fargo mused.

He spotted three barefoot boys fishing with long poles at

the edge of a good-size stream, then later saw a half dozen boys diving into a river. Missouri didn't lack for trees. The state had a wide range of hardwoods, from oak to ash and hickory and even some bald cypress in the wetter areas.

Fargo closed his eyes and took a short nap. The train whistle woke him, and he looked outside and saw mile marker eighty-eight flash past. He got the cleat planks ready to reach the four-foot drop to the ground. He could jump the Ovaro out, but he wasn't sure what kind of footing there would be beside the tracks.

The train began slowing a few minutes later, and Fargo saw the next mile marker come up. The train coasted a hundred yards shy of the marker, where there was a nearly level spot. The brakeman directed the engineer to the exact spot and the train stopped. Fargo put down the four cleated planks to give the Ovaro room to walk on. Then he was off the train and gone, riding three hundred yards back along the way they had come. He heard the train start up and pull away, heading on eastward. Fargo moved onto the side of the right-of-way, walking the pinto, checking and evaluating every clump of bushes and grass that grew on the right-hand bank. The train tracks burrowed their way through a solid stand of cottonwood and maples with a few elms in the fringes.

The country here was similar to most of the northern half of Missouri: gentle hills, open fertile plains, and well-watered prairies. This stretch included one of the rolling hills and a sharp gully to the left. The train was on an upward slope here and probably was not at full speed during the robbery, Fargo decided.

This was the country of the coneflower and larkspur, of deer and elk, bear and still some bison here and there, with otter and beaver in the rivers.

He was truly in his element. He knew about the plains and the woods. He could interpret the signs on the land, of the bushes, the wind, and the very earth itself. He had developed a special sensitivity to the land and its animals and plants. It kept him alive, it enabled him to track and trail men and animals that few men in the nation could. Fargo had learned to be a part of all nature, yet he was still able to draw back from it and interpret it and use it, much as the Indian had learned to do over the centuries. He could live as one with nature, but not be limited to it.

Fargo picked out a deer trail that crossed the tracks and vanished into the heavy growth of mixed cottonwood and maple. To one side he found the skeleton of a deer that might have been hit by a fast-moving train. Nothing else disturbed the natural growth along the tracks. He rode slowly, covering each square foot of ground twice.

At the eighty-seven-mile marker he paused and let his gaze take in the long view up and down the side of the tracks. He wasn't sure he was even on the right side of the rails. The express cars had doors that opened on both sides, depending on the station's platform. The robbers could have jumped either way.

Maybe. The mile markers were on this side. The robbers would have watched for the marker and probably opened the door on the left as the train moved up the grade. He viewed the scene ahead of him with long sweeping gazes, and stared hard at an area about thirty yards down the tracks. He spotted marks in the grass, weeds, and small bushes, and rode quickly to the spot, still checking the area from the marker to the damaged area.

As he came closer, Fargo could see definite marks showing where something had disturbed the natural growth of the grass and weeds. One small bush had been bent over and broken off, as if a man had crashed down the slope. He dismounted and studied the area again. A one-eyed man in a thunderstorm could find this spot. The heavy tracks of two men moved into the elm and sweet gum twenty yards from the tracks. From the sign it looked like the men had lain there for some time, then moved on downhill.

Fargo whistled for the Ovaro, which pranced down the right-of-way on easy footing, then down the bank where Fargo waited. He slapped the animal on the neck and rubbed his ears, then mounted. Skye could follow this blind man's trail from the saddle.

The track led downgrade for a half mile, working past more stands of cottonwood and maple, then followed a gully that emptied into a small valley with a stream in it. He saw where the men had hunkered down behind some bushes. They had set down four heavy bags. All had made plain impressions in the soft ground.

A new smell tingled Fargo's nostrils. A foreign scent that had nothing to do with the surrounding natural elements. A wisp of smoke from an almost dead campfire. He turned and sniffed again. The scent came from upstream. He studied the ground. The two men's footprints went across some loose sand and up along the bank of the stream.

Suddenly the tracks were gone. Fargo rode back ten feet and read the trail again. He hadn't seen them turn to the left into the stream. The pinto waded across the water that was only two feet deep at the center. The tracks showed on the far side and continued upstream.

Fargo caught another whiff of the campfire. He looked ahead and saw the blackened scar of charcoal on the brown sand of the streambank. The tracks led directly toward it.

Fargo worked forward, then circled the campfire, studying the sign left there. He figured there were four men. Two with cowboy boot heels, another one with a slightly wider heel, and a fourth with town shoes, broad sole and heel. Four men, two met by two. The pungent smell of coffee filtered through the noontime air. He could see where splashes of the liquid had put out most of the fire.

He identified two different sets of hoofprints. Both were

shod, and both had been in place for some time, with droppings sprinkling where they probably were ground-tied.

In one spot the cowboy boots seemed to be facing the tracks of the town-shoe man. The marks were three feet apart, aimed exactly at the other one. Just behind the boot prints, Fargo saw the heavy and wide mark of what could be a man's body stretched in the dirt. He found a dark reddish-brown spot he was sure was blood. Another blood stain showed almost two feet above that. Nearby he saw what had to be a part of a human skull with hair still attached.

Near the fire, Fargo found another place where a body could have dropped into the dirt. There was no blood here. A plain trail gouged into the dirt showed where both bodies had been dragged into the edge of the hickory and short-leaf pine trees twenty feet from the campfire.

Fargo stopped at the edge of the trees. With signs pointing to two dead bodies, and no circling buzzards or hawks, Fargo knew there were two shallow graves nearby. There was no sign of the mail sacks or any Railway Express items.

One body had been dragged through a six-foot-wide carpet of goldenrod and wild asters. The trail led under the short-leaf pines and up a slight slope about thirty feet under the trees when it ended. Someone had tried to conceal the grave by throwing branches and some grass and forest mulch on top of the newly turned earth.

He went back to the campfire and found the other drag trail, which led along the stream bank for fifty feet before it turned sharply into the pines and ending at a second grave ten feet inside the tree line. Fargo dropped to his knees at the edge of the dug-up earth. He had to know. He found a broken-off branch and used it to loosen the soil. Then he scooped it out with his hands. He worked one end, hoping it was the right one.

A foot down, he unearthed a hand. He worked more carefully as he dug around it. Then another six inches down he came to the head. He removed just enough of the dirt and leaves to get a firm description of the body, then covered it up again.

At the second grave, Fargo hit the wrong end and came up with cowboy boots. He went to the other end of the grave and soon had the second man's head exposed. This one was more distinctive, with lots of red hair and fair skin. He also had a scar on his left cheek.

The Trailsman covered the second body, memorized the spot where he was, and whistled for the Ovaro. It trotted up to Fargo and stood in front of him. Fargo mounted the pinto and rode back to trace the horseshoe prints. There seemed to be a mishmash of tracks, and he had to circle the fire at fifty feet to nail down the double set of prints that headed west toward Plainview. Fargo wondered if the two killers would go all the way through the trees and brush, or would they branch off toward the old stage road and head east away from the town?

Ten minutes later, Fargo had one question answered. He came across a litter of paper under the trees. He dismounted and checked it and knew it was the registered mail. They had even left the two heavy burlap postal bags. Fargo stared at the trashed mail for a full minute, then bent down and began to pick up the papers and letters and stuff them into one of the burlap bags.

It took him two hours to gather up all of the pieces of paper and envelopes and torn-up letters on the forest floor. The torn-up mail was scattered out more than a hundred feet, and he did most of it on his hands and knees. The torn-up paper took more room than the original mail had, and Fargo had to cram the last pieces into the sacks to get everything inside. He tied the bags together, circled the ropes around his chest, and let the bags hang down his back. Better than spooking the Ovaro with the clumsy things banging on his hindquarters for twenty-four more miles.

An hour later, he was still tracking the pair of mounts,

heading up a long valley to the west that would come out near the railroad and the stage road beyond it.

The trail had wound higher, and Fargo checked the sun through the canopy of sweet gum and elm. He figured it should be a little after three in the afternoon. Then he remembered his pocket watch and pulled it out on its rawhide leash and opened the front. The watch showed 3:10. What did he need a watch for? He brayed a laugh and grinned.

Another hour of easy tracking and he came to the railroad. The pair of riders had paused there and let their mounts eat some of the new grass. Then they had crossed the tracks and headed due north for the old stage road. When the riders had paused beside the road, one of the horses relieved itself. Skye stepped down from his mount and felt the horse biscuits. They were no longer warm. In this weather they would cool down in about four hours. He had to be at least five, maybe six hours behind the pair. No chance he could catch them before they hit Plainview—if they were going there, and if they didn't stop for the night somewhere. If they had camped, he would have a chance to catch them.

Fargo kneed the Ovaro into a canter. He could cover six miles in an hour this way. A walking horse covered four. It was easy riding on the old stagecoach road. A few small trees had taken root and lots of grass and shrubs had sprung up, but there were few washouts and no fallen-down bridges. A little after five-thirty he pulled up the pinto to a walk.

Fargo dug out some beef jerky and chewed on a slab. The dried beef would provide him with enough energy to keep him going for several days. He had another two hours of light before he'd have to decide what to do. He would ride into the night, or stop for some sleep and head on in tomorrow.

At seven-thirty, he decided he had about ten more miles to town. He'd ride on. He moved the mail bags to a pack in back of his saddle and rode on. With any luck he should hit town just about ten o'clock. The café would still be open, which would be a welcome change from the jerky.

It was 9:50 when Fargo rode up to the post office and swung down the two Railway Express bags. Two men came out of the shadows and pounced on the bags. One held up a silver badge Fargo had never seen before.

"Larson, U.S. postal inspector. We were almost here when we heard about the robbery. Those the bags?"

"Right. The mail is ripped up and tattered, but I found every shred. Gonna be a patchwork puzzle."

"That's my job. I have help and a room with big tables. We'll be working around the clock until we put it back together. We have the register logs from the last clerk. We'll check it off and see if anything is missing."

"It's all yours." Fargo turned and led the pinto to the Farm Home Café. He wanted a huge steak, three baked potatoes, a bucket of gravy, and all the coffee he could guzzle. He took his time eating, savoring every bite. After he paid the check, he put the Ovaro in the stable and had it wiped down and fed.

As Fargo came out of the livery, two men watched him from the shadows in front of a saloon across the street.

"So he found the mail sacks. We figured somebody would. Don't hurt us a bit." The larger of the two men spoke softly. He wore an expensive suit, and a gold chain linked his vest pockets. In the center of the chain hung a gold nugget the size of a marble.

"Somebody had to go look for it," the second man said. "That's about all the good it's going to do them." He was rail thin and wore a brown suit and black bowler. He touched snuff to his nose and summarily sneezed. "That is absolutely all that mister railroad detective is going to learn," the thin man said with a touch of authority. "If he wants to stay healthy, that better be all he digs up about this little matter of the train robbery."